"I Can't Be

"Yes!" Sobs we~~~~ ~~~~~~ ~~~ ~~~~~~, making the words ragged and uneven. "Yes, you were mistaken. I was mistaken to let you . . . to allow you to think . . ." She broke off, gulped for air, then continued, "I don't want you, Doug Farrell! Not ever, do you hear me? Not ever!"

With the speed of lightning, Doug was off the bed and on his feet. His dark eyes glinted like burning coals. "I guess," he grated harshly, "I did make a mistake after all. I had begun to think I wanted you forever . . . as my wife!"

He turned, and an instant later he was gone.

SONDRA STANFORD

fell in love with the written word as soon as she could read one, at the age of six. However, besides her writing ability, she is also a gifted painter, and it was a "struggle to decide which talent would dominate." Fortunately for all her Silhouette readers, the written word triumphed.

Dear Reader:

Silhouette Books is pleased to announce the creation of a new line of contemporary romances—*Silhouette Special Editions*. Each month we'll bring you six new love stories written by the best of today's authors—Janet Dailey, Brooke Hastings, Laura Hardy, Sondra Stanford, Linda Shaw, Patti Beckman, and many others.

Silhouette Special Editions are written with American women in mind; they are for readers who want more: more story, more details and descriptions, more realism, and more *romance*. *Special Editions* are longer than most contemporary romances allowing for a closer look at the relationship between hero and heroine with emphasis on heightened romantic tension and greater sensuous and sensual detail. If you want more from a romance, be sure to look for *Silhouette Special Editions* on sale this February wherever you buy books.

We welcome any suggestions or comments, and I invite you to write us at the address below.

Karen Solem
Editor-in-Chief
Silhouette Books
P.O. Box 769
New York, N. Y. 10019

SONDRA STANFORD
Whisper Wind

Silhouette *Romance*
Published by Silhouette Books New York
America's Publisher of Contemporary Romance

Other Silhouette Romances by Sondra Stanford

And Then Came Dawn
Golden Tide
Long Winter's Night
No Trespassing

Shadow of Love
Storm's End
Yesterday Shadow

SILHOUETTE BOOKS, a Simon & Schuster Division of
GULF & WESTERN CORPORATION
1230 Avenue of the Americas, New York, N.Y. 10020

Distributed by Pocket Books

ISBN: 0-671-57112-5

First Silhouette Books printing November, 1981

10 9 8 7 6 5 4 3 2 1

All of the characters in this book are fictitious. Any resemblance to actual persons, living or dead, is purely coincidental.

Map by Tony Ferrara

America's Publisher of Contemporary Romance

Printed in the U.S.A.

*For Huey, with thanks
for his unwavering support*

WYOMING

NEBRASKA

KANSAS

UTAH

Fort Collins ●

Vail ●

Lucky ●

★ Denver

Pikes Peak ●
Colorado Springs ●

N
W ─┼─ E
S

COLORADO

Places set in italics are fictitious.

ARIZONA

NEW MEXICO

OKLAHOMA

Chapter One

Agnes Hart drew the Ford to a halt before the hospital entrance and got out. She smiled encouragingly at the pale, thin girl who waited in a wheelchair. "Ready?"

Sara Scott nodded and rose to her feet while the nurse who had come outside with her handed her bags to Agnes to stow in the trunk. Sara smiled and held out her hand to the nurse. "Thanks so much for everything," she said earnestly. "I almost feel like I'm leaving my family."

"We all feel the same way about you," the nurse smiled warmly. "Take good care of yourself."

"I will," Sara promised. She turned and limped painfully toward the passenger side of the car and awkwardly slid her long, slender blue-jean covered legs inside.

A moment later the car swept away from the curb. Sara waved back at the nurse and happily expelled a long sigh. At last she was leaving the hospital! It was almost like a dream come true and she gazed out the window with keen appreciation. It was a beautiful clear day in May and though she had spent months here, this was her first real glimpse of Colorado Springs. Today the world was bright and sunny, awash with the promise of summer. Pikes Peak, with its topping of snow, basked grandly in the golden light against the blue sky.

It was not until they were on the interstate headed north that Agnes spoke. But when she did, her voice was thick with concern. "Are you sure you're strong enough for this, Sara? Maybe the doctor was right and you should have stayed a few more weeks."

Sara shook her head vigorously. "No way! I feel as though I've just been let out of prison. Almost five months! That was winter. There was snow when I went in and now look—the world is fresh and new again!"

Agnes smiled. "You have had a rough time of it, honey. I just hope this mountain cabin will be good for your recuperation."

"I know it will," Sara said firmly. "And I really appreciate everything you've done." Her lips quivered. There was just no adequate way to express her gratitude. Agnes had been a tower of strength ever since the accident, making numerous flying trips out from Los Angeles, seeing to all her business arrangements, closing up her apartment, storing her furniture, finding and leasing this mountain cabin for her, even purchasing this car. Agnes had relentlessly tended to the endless hospital details and had given her all the moral support she had so desperately needed just to get through the long ordeal. No, there was no way she could ever convey how much it had all meant to her.

"I've been glad to do it," Agnes told her in a gruff voice. "Well, some of it, anyway. But I still think you're making a mistake in not coming straight back to L.A. Your career—"

"Is finished," Sara said abruptly. "Let's not rehash it, okay?"

Agnes' mouth lost some of its sternness as her dark eyes swept across the wan face opposite her. "I'll let it go for now," she relented, "but not for good, so you needn't think you're getting off totally

8

free. When you're stronger, we're going to fight this thing out."

Sara grinned, shook her head and reached out to turn the knob on the radio. A popular male singer's voice filled the airwaves and she relaxed against the seat, idly observing Agnes' profile from beneath her lowered gold-tipped lashes.

It was strange, really, the close relationship the two of them had developed. It was actually more like that of mother and daughter rather than that of agent and singer. Agnes was forty-plus, with short, dark hair, lightly peppered with gray. Unlike the glamorous people she dealt with daily, she disdained artificial measures of youth and beauty for herself and only wore a light coating of lipstick. Though her manner was often gruff and forbidding, it had somehow never deceived Sara for an instant. Sara loved Agnes dearly, just as Agnes' husband Walter had adored her until his death two years ago. Four years ago, Agnes had heard Sara sing, signed her on as a client and that same year her first single had been recorded. Shortly after it had been released, Sara's mother had died of a long-term heart ailment and Agnes and Walter Hart had taken Sara under their wings, treating her as the child they had never had. Ever since, the relationship had endured, far surpassing a mere professional affiliation.

A moment later, Sara's peace was shattered when she heard the radio announcer's voice. "And here's one I know you'll enjoy . . . Sheila Starr singing the last song Pete Brewster wrote for her before his untimely death last year in an airplane crash that also injured Sheila. Let's listen now to 'Forever Our Love.'"

As the first note of the music began, Sara sat upright, alarmingly pale. With a jerking, convulsive movement, she switched off the radio and the car was suddenly filled with a tense silence.

"I thought," Agnes said after a long moment, "you told me you could cope with life now. But if this is how you're going to behave every time you hear one of your own songs—"

"I know," Sara choked out. "I'm being ridiculous. It was just the shock . . . hearing it so suddenly like that, and the announcer mentioning Pete and the accident."

"Honey," Agnes said gently, "you're making everything unbearably hard on yourself. Why don't you give up this cabin idea? I don't like your being out there all alone. Come back home with me. Rest up and get your strength back, certainly. But then face the reporters, pick up the pieces of your life and start over again. Hiding out from the world doesn't solve anything. Besides, nobody's forgotten you. Your public is—"

Sara shook her head and ran an agitated hand through her short-cropped blonde hair. Her blue eyes were swimming in tears and her voice quivered as she said, "It's Sheila Starr's public, not mine, not anymore. Face facts, Agnes! I've got a limp now and I don't look the same since the plastic surgery. The career I had is over. If I tried to go back now, people would only feel sorry for me and I don't want pity."

"Then why not stop pitying yourself?" Agnes said tartly. Sara opened her mouth to deny it, but Agnes forestalled her. "Yes, that's exactly what you're doing, Sara. Maybe you're not as stunningly beautiful as you once were, but you're still very lovely, thanks to an extremely skilled plastic surgeon. That blonde hair of yours will grow back in time and the limp will gradually lessen. So what if you don't look the same? It's your voice people come to hear in concert and it's your voice that makes them buy your records. Is this really what you think Pete would have wanted you to do—bury yourself out here in the mountain wilderness and declare that your career is over for good? Would he have done it if it had been you who had died instead?"

"I don't know," Sara said wearily. "I don't know anything anymore." Again she leaned back against the seat and closed her eyes. The question was moot, anyway. Pete *was* dead instead of her, and besides, a songwriter's career was different. He wouldn't have had to face the glare of publicity like she would.

She opened her eyes again and gazed silently out the window at the blurred countryside. Agnes was at least right about one thing, she thought. She had to get a grip on herself now that she was again in the outside world. Breaking down because she heard her name over the radio was merely proving Agnes' point that she should still be in the hospital. Shifting her position in the seat, she turned and smiled at the older woman. "Tell me about the cabin," she commanded. "Exactly where is it?"

"About fifty miles out of Denver," Agnes answered. "The nearest community is a little place called Lucky. The cabin is about seven miles out, but Lucky Creek runs just below it. I think you'll like it."

"Lucky Creek?" Sara added musingly.

Agnes chuckled. "Actually, Unlucky Creek would be a better name. Lucky was a little mining town that grew up around the creek during the gold rush."

"Not one of the more successful ventures, I gather?" Sara asked.

"Oh, they managed to get some gold out of the stream, I understand, but nothing like the deposits found at Clear Creek or California Gulch."

"What's the cabin like?"

"Simple and rustic," Agnes stated succinctly, "but comfortable. It's got a living room, two bedrooms, a small kitchen and bath. A fireplace, too."

"Sounds lovely," Sara murmured approvingly. "What about the view?"

Agnes grinned and shook her head. "I'll let you decide that for yourself."

They reached the cabin shortly after two that afternoon. The pines and blue spruces hid it from view of the narrow, rocky unpaved road. It was set atop a small hill and from behind the cabin there was a clear view of Lucky Creek winding its way downhill from the mountains. Beyond the creek in the distance were the glorious, majestic Rocky Mountains, still topped with winter snow. Spruces, pines and aspens clung tenaciously to the mountainsides and far above the timberline, Sara spotted the jeweled green glint of a lake.

She took a deep breath, turned to Agnes and gave her an impulsive hug. "You're an angel to find me such a heavenly place to stay. I'm going to love it here."

"I'm glad you approve," Agnes said in a brisk voice. "But now let's get your things inside. I ordered a taxi in Lucky to be here for me by four and I want to help you get settled in a little before I leave."

The cabin was small but well laid out and comfortably furnished. The living room boasted a rock fireplace and in front of it lay a bright orange rug. Pine paneling made the room homey and an Indian blanket lay across the back of the white sofa. Its bold geometric design provided a vivid splash of color. In one corner of the room stood a piano. When she saw it, Sara whirled around toward Agnes. "You had it sent out?" Her voice held an accusation. "Why? I *told* you distinctly I didn't want it."

Agnes shrugged and refused to meet her eyes. "I thought it might be company to you on cold, lonely nights. And while we're at it, your stereo and albums are in the spare bedroom."

"Agnes!"

"I know, you'd like to bite my head off. If you want to, go right ahead. But like I told you in the car, you can't just bury the past completely, Sara. You are what you are and music is important to you. You might as well face up to it a little at a time."

Sara's shoulders drooped in defeat. "I suppose maybe you're right," she agreed reluctantly. "At least I know you did it to help me."

"That's right, I did," Agnes said firmly. "Now take a look in the kitchen. I laid in a stock of groceries for you. Why don't we make some coffee right now?"

Two hours later, Sara was alone. The taxi had arrived and carried Agnes to Lucky where she would catch a bus for Denver, then a flight back to Los Angeles and her busy job that she had neglected far too much in favor of Sara these past few months.

This was what she wanted, Sara told herself as she gazed about the quiet living room—privacy, solitude and anonymity. But now that she actually had them she wasn't at all sure if she had made the right decision after all.

She ate an early supper of soup and crackers, took a hot bath and in her nightgown and robe, curled up on the sofa with a book. But instead of opening it, she stared unseeingly at the cold, dark cavern of the fireplace and thought about Pete and about the past that was gone forever, just as he was.

Poor Pete, such a bright lamp, extinguished far too early. She still missed him dreadfully at times. He had always been such a fun-loving person, although now she wondered with wistful sadness whether or not she would ever have married him. She had loved him as a good friend but she had always known she didn't love him the way a wife should love a husband. But she had never had a chance to give him her answer. He had made his impulsive proposal that morning when they had left Aspen in his private plane. They had been skiing with friends and had decided to visit another of Pete's friends in Colorado Springs before heading back to California the next day. When he suggested they get married and she had realized that he was really serious, she had told him she would need time to think it over. Pete had laughed and said she could have all the time she wanted so long as her answer was "yes" and she gave it to him by nightfall. Only there had been no nightfall for Pete. They had run into a sudden snow storm and the plane had crashed.

There was a sudden crashing now. The pounding noise jolted Sara out of her reverie. For an instant she was totally disoriented before she realized someone was knocking insistently on the door.

She struggled to her feet and limped across the room. When she pulled open the door, her mind first registered a vague surprise that nighttime had fallen. Then as her eyes focused on the man who stood before her, a sudden shock overcame her. Sara swayed and if she had not been clutching the door knob, she would have fallen.

The man's hair was as dark as the forest night and his eyes were two black coals. His face was angular and a cleft was chisled into his chin. His broad shoulders amply filled his black casual pullover shirt. A pleasant smile hovered on his lips, but almost immediately it vanished and the mouth became a straight line of uncompromising grimness while his thick dark brows suddenly crushed low over his eyes.

"Miss Scott?" His voice was cold, but there was also an element of surprise beneath the iciness of it.

Sara's golden head bobbed up and down as she swallowed hard. Her mouth felt dry and she could not have spoken a word just then if her life had depended on it.

14

"My name's Farrell," he said in a clipped tone. "I'm your landlord. May I come in for a moment?"

Again Sara nodded and she backed away a step or two so that he could enter. All at once she became aware of her apparel and began tugging nervously at the overlapping ends of her white robe, trying to make sure she was well covered.

The man closed the door, shutting out the sharp chill of the mountain night air and then he turned to face her. His gaze went immediately to her fumbling hands where they gripped the robe together between her breasts and a hateful expression of amusement flickered in his eyes.

"Don't worry." His voice was scornful. "I didn't come here to rape you."

Sara flinched beneath his ugly words and her face went a deathly pale. Limply, her arms fell to her sides as she mustered all the dignity she had at her command.

"I didn't suppose you did, Mr. Farrell." Her voice was thick and wispy, not at all related to her natural, clear tone. But then anger strengthened it. "What *did* you come about?"

His head was cocked to one side while his eyes studied her face in minute detail and for a moment he did not reply. Sara stood breathless under his searching scrutiny and prayed that he could not hear the erratic thumping of her heart.

"You look very familiar to me somehow," he said at last. "Have we met before?"

A chill swept up her spine and a slight flush stained her cheeks. *Dear heaven*, she thought, *let me carry this off*. She gave a disdainful shrug and her lips curled into a mocking smile. "Oh, come now, Mr. Farrell," she taunted with calculated deliberation, "surely you know *that* line is as old as these mountains?"

A dark angry expression crossed his face and his

coal-black eyes glittered dangerously. He took a menancing step toward her. "Is that what you think . . . that I'm trying to come on to you?"

"Aren't you?" Sara flung back recklessly.

"Hardly," A sneer twisted his mouth. "You're quite lovely in your own way, I suppose," he conceded as his hard eyes raked mercilessly over her body, "but to tell the truth, I prefer my women to have a little more flesh on their bones. You're a bit too skinny for my taste and why any woman with lovely platinum-blond hair would want to chop it off so close to her scalp beats me." He shook his head in a puzzled fashion as his critical gaze surveyed her short locks before his eyes met hers once more. "But there is something about you that reminds me of someone I must have met or seen before," he insisted.

Sara gave a light shrug to her shoulders and half turned, so that she was no longer directly facing those keen, intelligent eyes. "They say we all have a twin somewhere in the world," she commented as casually as she could manage. "But now," her voice chilled, "that you're through taking inventory, do you mind telling me why you came?"

"You're Agnes Hart's friend?"

His abrupt question surprised Sara and she turned once more to face him. "Yes, of course. Why?"

His mouth set into a grim line. "There's been a mistake, Miss Scott, and I'd appreciate it if you would leave tomorrow."

Sara gasped and stared at him with disbelief. "Leave? I just signed a six-month lease!"

"I'm as well aware of that as you are," he responded, "but Agnes represented you to me under false pretenses. She said she wanted this place for a friend who has been ill and needs a quiet place to recuperate. I thought she meant someone her own age, of course."

Sara's eyes flashed her anger back at his. "What does my age have to do with anything?" she demanded.

"Plenty. Your age, your looks, your sex." His gaze was penetrating as he once again scrutinized her face. "How old are you anyway, about nineteen or twenty?"

"I'm almost twenty-four, if it happens to be any of your business, which I don't see that it is," Sara said indignantly. "But why should you want me out of here because of that?"

"What you're bound to be looking for is excitement, parties and the like," he pointed out reasonably, just as though he were trying to explain to a four-year-old child why she shouldn't play in the middle of the street. "I've got enough on my hands without coping with a lot of loud noise and destruction to my property, not to mention worrying about the safety of a single young woman living here alone. My realty agent will refund your deposit and reimburse your moving expenses as soon as you move out."

"Is that so?" Sara was suddenly trembling with an all-consuming rage. Her eyes darkened like a threatening storm cloud illuminated by lightning. Her stature was dwarfed by the immense height of the man who towered over her, but she was not about to allow herself to be intimidated. She drew her shoulders back and lifted her head proudly so that her delicately-shaped chin jutted out. "I'm an adult who certainly doesn't need you to worry about my living here alone. I can take care of myself quite adequately, thank you. Also," now her voice hardened into chunks of ice, "I happen to have signed a six-month lease agreement which I fully intend to utilize. If you want me out, you're going to have to take me to court!"

For a long moment it was a standoff as they glared

at one another and then the man growled in a low, savage voice, "So, you're a troublemaker already, are you?"

"If I have to be," Sara acknowledged with angry determination. "For the next six months this cabin belongs to me and if I want to throw parties, there's nothing you can do about it. Goodnight, *Mr. Farrell*," she ended frigidly, with a faint emphasis upon his name. "I have nothing further to say to you."

For another endless moment they watched each other, her tempestous blue eyes clashing with his smouldering black ones. Hostility vibrated throughout the room.

At last Sara's unwelcome visitor broke the tense silence between them. "You've not heard the last from me on this subject, Miss Scott, believe me. You're not welcome here!" Then, with stunning speed, he turned, opened the door and went out, slamming the door behind him.

Like a dazed sleepwalker, Sara moved toward the door where she slipped the bolt. Then, without any awareness of what she was doing, she returned to her former position on the sofa. As she sat down, her abandoned book slid unheeded from the sofa to the floor as her mind grappled with the shock it had just been dealt.

Doug! How could it be possible that he, of all people in the world, should turn out to be her new landlord? A trembling hand went up to touch her quivering lips. Oh God, it was dreadful and despite what she had told him, she would have to leave at once. She couldn't possibly stay here now.

Her hand left her mouth and lowered slowly to her lap. Sara stared at the knotted fist as though seeing it for the first time. It was her injured hand, the one which was still too weak to be of much use, although it, like her leg, would be perfectly normal in time according to the doctors. But it was what the hand reminded her of now that held her thoughts. She no longer looked the same! That was why Doug had not recognized her, even though he had noticed something familiar about her.

She rose again and went into the bedroom, flipping on the overhead light before going to stand before the mirror. For endless months after the accident she had not been allowed to look into a mirror, and after the operations began her face had been swathed in bandages much of the time. Only for the past month or so had she at last been allowed to view her new self. Though she had begun to adjust to the change, the subtly different face that met her eyes whenever she glanced into a mirror was not one to attract her attention to the point where she ever studied it long.

Now, however, she studied it intently, with new eyes and a curious detachment. What was it about her that had touched off a chord of memory in Doug's mind? Certainly at a casual glance, no one would associate her with the glamorous singing personality, Sheila Starr. Sara would have been stupid not to know that before the accident she had been beautiful. She had been told it often enough by adoring fans, photographers and men. Even Doug, she thought painfully. Then she had had long, flowing blonde hair that had waved and billowed around her shoulders, wide blue eyes fringed by smoky gray lashes and a dimple in her cheek when she smiled. Well, she still had the blonde hair, but as Doug had so cruelly pointed out, it was extremely short, now curling and waving snugly against her head. It had grown enough to be stylishly "cute," but even so Sara hated it. It altered her looks as radically as had the surgery.

She leaned toward the mirror for a closer inspection. Though she still had the blue eyes and even the dimple, there was no way in the world that she could kid herself that she was still beautiful. Her nose was smaller now, her cheekbones not so prominent as before, her chin more delicately rounded. Her face had been crushed badly in the plane crash and there had been several operations before the present state had been achieved. Even now, searching critically she could see the tiny red line of a scar beneath the chin and on the side of her head through her hair. No, she was definitely not Sheila Starr any longer. Now she was just plain Sara Scott again. A skinny Sara Scott at that, she thought wryly, recalling Doug's wounding words tonight. And he had been right. She looked like a scarecrow, all angles and bones protruding instead of gentle curves. No, she shouldn't be at all surprised that he hadn't recognized her. In all honesty, it would have been more astounding if he had.

Sara was thankful that when she had first begun her career she had not used her own name on the stage. "Sheila Starr" had been an invention of her mother's because Sara Scott had sounded so ordinary. At the time Sara had thought it was silly, but had gone along with it and now she was devoutly grateful. Doug had known Sheila, not Sara, and tonight she had been spared the humiliation and embarrassment she would have suffered if he had recognized her name.

With a muffled cry of frustration, Sara whirled away from the mirror, unable to bear for another instant the haunted expression that clouded her eyes. Why had a capricious fate brought her back into contact with a man she had known less than a week but who had hurt her so deeply she had never been able to totally forget him?

During the past three years she had done her best to put Doug Farrell as completely out of her thoughts as he was out of her life. And her life had been filled to overflowing during that time—

recording sessions, concerts, tours and other men as well. Gradually the hurt had lessened, the spaces of time when she didn't think of him lengthened until she only spared him an occasional brief thought, usually whenever she had happened to see another man who reminded her of him. Finally, she had truly believed herself wholly free from him at last. Until tonight.

Tonight Doug had angrily blamed Agnes for tricking him into leasing the cabin to her friend whom he had assumed was Agnes' own age. Now, for the first time, Sara wondered too, whether it had been deliberately intentional.

Wearily, she gave her head a negative shake and sank down onto the edge of the bed. The suspicion was without foundation. She knew that with absolute certainty even though, ironically, it had been in Agnes' home where she had first met Doug.

Sara gazed at the window opposite the bed as the memory of that night returned with crystal clearness. Agnes and Walter's house had overflowed with guests from both the entertainment and business world: the tinkling sound of ice in glasses; the murmur of voices; the haze of cigarette smoke; the gaily-colored Japanese lanterns that lit the patio and garden; the glitter of the multicolored lights on the water in the swimming pool. And Sara had been dressed in a floor-length gold dress that had made her feel like a fairy princess.

Princess. That was the very name Doug had used to christen her. Sara's heart lurched as the memories flooded into the present.

She had been barely twenty-one at the time; Doug a mature thirty-two. That had been the whole root of the problem, she thought now. She had been too young and immature to handle a relationship with a man like him. Although her mother had aggressively promoted her singing career, she had given Sara a very sheltered upbringing. Although she appeared to be glamorous and even had a budding career, the truth was that she was in no way prepared for the realities of the world, especially when it came to man/woman relationships. She had liked to imagine that she was as enlightened and sophisticated as the next young woman of today, but when the chips were down, she had failed the test abysmally. But then, she told herself bitterly now, what could you expect from a mere "princess?" Only queens knew their way around.

They had met outside the house, in the Hart's lovely garden near the pool, and Doug had walked straight up to her, smiled and said, "Hello, Princess. Where are all your minions?"

"What are you talking about?" she had asked in puzzlement.

"As lovely as you are, you must have dozens of servile followers. Or are all the men in L.A. blind?"

Sara had laughed and Doug had laughed with her and that had been the beginning. They had sat together in a secluded, dark corner of the back lawn for some time talking and then later Doug had driven her home to her apartment where they had spent another two hours talking over coffee. She had learned that he lived in Colorado, owned an electronics company, loved mountains and steak smothered in onions and gravy. She had told him of her first record, which was at that moment on all the hit charts, of her sadness since her mother's death a few months earlier and of her love for the ocean and charm bracelets. When Doug had left that night, he had kissed her briefly but warmly and they had made a date for the following day.

What an idyllic time they had had during the next two days, Sara thought now. She lay back against the pillows on the bed and gave full rein to her retrospective thoughts. They had gone to the beach together, had dined and danced and Doug had even bought her a new charm to add to one of her bracelets—a small golden heart with the letter D engraved upon it. She still had the charm, tucked away in her jewelry case, but she had never been able to bring herself to attach it to a bracelet and wear it. Not after the way things had ended.

The weekend had followed their two days together in the city. Doug had had access to a friend's cabin in the mountains and he had invited Sara to spend the weekend with him there. She had accepted without hesitation and had gone with eyes wide open, knowing what was to come. Yet she had welcomed it because in only two short days she had known herself to be wildly, joyfully, wholeheartedly and unashamedly in love.

They had driven up on Saturday morning and the day had been lovely. After settling in they had carried a picnic basket down to a nearby lake for lunch. Doug had even brought a bottle of wine along. Again Doug had talked about his business and his dislike of traveling, which was a necessary part of his work. Sara, who was preparing for a second concert tour the following week, could share his distaste of a steady diet of lonely hotel rooms and restaurant meals. Later, they had gone for a hike halfway up a mountain trail and when Doug had kissed her in that rarified atmosphere, Sara had pretended to swoon and they had broken into laughter again. Looking back, Sara thought sadly, it had seemed as if they had always been laughing together.

The lighthearted laughter had continued when, back at the cabin, they had prepared their dinner together as darkness fell. Even knowing what went later, Sara could still smile while remembering how she had been pouring stew into a bowl when Doug had accidentally bumped her arm and some of it had spilled onto the floor. She had exclaimed, "Thunderation and tarnation!" before stooping to wipe it up. Doug had chuckled about such dreadful "sailor cussing" before he, too, had stooped to help her clean the mess and had ended up pulling her into his arms and kissing her again.

But then everything had gone sour. As the evening wore on, Sara had become nervous. She drank too much wine in an effort to regain her faltering courage and she had grown jumpy at Doug's slightest touch. But she comforted herself that he didn't notice anything amiss and when at last he had suggested she go upstairs and get ready for bed first, she had had to force herself to make each step.

She could still feel the chilling darkness of that bedroom after she had turned out the lights and had lain huddled beneath the blankets as she had waited for Doug. She could still recall the terror that had possessed her when he had come at last and had lain down beside her.

Gently, he had pulled her into his arms and then an instant later, he had exclaimed in a shocked voice, "You're trembling as though you're ill, Princess! What is it?"

The tears had come then, and touching her wet face in the darkness, Doug had sworn viciously under his breath and had snapped on the bedside lamp.

Sara shuddered now at the volcanic anger that had erupted. With quick, probing questions, Doug had arrived at the truth—that it was her first experience at being with a man. But instead of being pleased about it he had been furious. He had demanded to know why she had accepted his invitation, knowing what it had implied. When she tearfully told him that she was in love with him, he had sworn again, swung

24

his legs off the bed, donned a robe and had thrown hers at her. He had been enraged and his words, flung at her three years ago, still reverberated in her head.

"Love doesn't enter into it," he had said callously. "I don't believe in it. I also don't play around with little innocents! And what business do you have being a little innocent anyway? You're in show business! You're supposed to know your way around!" On and on had gone his angry tirade while Sara had crouched miserably on the bed, her robe clutched awkwardly in front of her before he had ordered her to dress so that he could drive her home.

The humiliation she had suffered at Doug's hands that night still had the power to shake her. She had determined at the time that no man would ever have the opportunity to hurt or embarrass her again as Doug had done, and it was a vow she had faithfully kept ever since. There had been many men whom she had dated during the last three years. Being in the public eye as she had been, there had been published reports of love affairs and near marriages. But the truth was that she had never let another man close to her in any meaningful way whatsoever, except for Pete. And with Pete it had been different. He had been her close friend and confidant, but never her lover, though he had wanted to be.

Sara stared up at the ceiling. Her entire body throbbed with pain as she discovered that she had never quite gotten over the blow Doug had dealt her.

How she wished that Pete was still alive! In that moment, she would have married him. But on the heels of that thought came her sensibility. Pete had been a dear friend, far too good to have been married to any woman seeking refuge. He had deserved more than that and now she realized that she could never have done that to him, even though he would have represented the safety she had so desperately needed.

Resolutely her mind returned to the real issue at hand. Doug *was* here. She was here. And what was she going to do now? *Run?* her numbed brain asked. *Yes, run.* Run fast and run far.

Chapter Two

There was a definite chill in the air when Sara awoke the following morning. Used as she was to the centrally-controlled heating of the hospital, she had given no thought to what it would be like in the cabin. Here there were only electric heaters and the fireplace, neither of which she had bothered with the night before.

She shivered as she flung back the bedcovers and scurried across the cold floor into the bathroom. There she made quick work of washing up and brushing her teeth before she rushed back to the bedroom and donned her jeans and a thick crimson sweater. Her short hair was hopeless and she stood in front of the mirror only as long as was absolutely necessary to run a quick brush through the tight curls. She didn't bother with makeup.

In the kitchen she made coffee and drank a cup while standing at the window. Then with an eagerness she hadn't experienced since she was a child, she headed outdoors and made her way downhill for her first close-up view of Lucky Creek.

By the time she reached the stream she was panting from the unaccustomed exertion and she sat down on a boulder to rest and catch her breath. Her leg still hurt when she walked and steep hills strained her muscles.

The water was sparkling like champagne as it

glinted in the sunlight. A little way downstream she spotted a beaver dam. A small chipmunk danced across the ground nearby, delighting her. It was so peaceful, so beautiful here that it seemed as though such a wonderful place should have magic powers to make life's troubles wash away. And for a little while, Sara let it do just that. She lifted her face to the warmth of the sunlight that filtered through the trees and basked in her new found freedom, refusing to allow her mind to dwell upon anything at all outside of this moment.

But presently, sharp hunger pains assailed her. With reluctance, she forced herself to rise and began the wearing, painful process of the uphill climb back to the cabin. The doctors had told her that walking was the best exercise she could give her left leg and she was grimly determined to follow that advice. So she bit her lip to stifle the moan that rose in her throat as she started her uphill trek.

When she reached level ground at the top of the hill, she paused to catch her breath again. About ten yards directly ahead was the cabin and as she glanced absently toward it, she was startled to see a blue pickup truck parked beside the cabin. A man with his back toward her was pulling something off of the bed of the truck.

With another quick gasp, Sara moved forward slowly, her limp now badly pronounced. She was still about five yards away when the man turned at last, his arms loaded with wood, and she recognized Doug.

This morning he was dressed in faded jeans, a western-style shirt and boots. He was the epitome of rugged, masculine self-sufficiency. His entire body was lean, rock-hard muscular strength. Though Sara knew he had seen her as he turned from the truck, he made no acknowledgment of her presence as he carried the load of wood to the side of the cabin where he dropped it on top of another pile. Then, without even glancing in her direction, he headed back to the truck for still another load.

By the time he returned, Sara was standing beside the woodpile. "What are you doing?" she asked as he dropped his burden and then began to dust off his hands.

His cool dark eyes met hers and his thick eyebrows lifted. "What does it look like I'm doing?" he countered.

"It looks like you're bringing me firewood."

Doug grinned and the flash of his teeth was startlingly white against the bronzed tone of his skin. "Bright girl!" he taunted. "You just might get an 'A' for observation."

Sara stiffened with indignation. "There's no need for you to be sarcastic," she snapped. "The question is why are you doing this?" She waved a hand toward the pile of split logs.

Doug shrugged his shoulders carelessly. "It was what I came to do last night," he told her. "To welcome Agnes' friend. But you made me so angry I forgot about it."

"I'm surprised you'd even bother since you told me to get out. Have you changed your mind already?"

Doug shook his head and grinned wickedly. "Oh no, I still don't want you here. But I decided there was no point in your freezing to death while you pack."

"And what makes you so sure I'm going to do that?" Sara bristled. "I told you I planned to stay. Have you decided to go ahead and take me to court?"

The grin on his face stretched wider. "No, I've just decided to let nature take its course."

"Meaning?"

"Meaning that I'll just wait until boredom and

loneliness get the better of you instead. I figure it can't be too long before you decide to head out for livelier places."

In spite of herself, Sara's lips twitched and then she burst out laughing. "Have you forgotten the wild, hell-raising parties I'm planning to throw?"

She won an answering smile from Doug. "Well now," he said with approval, "you can smile. I'd about decided you had never been taught. It's much more becoming to you than a frown."

"And who's been responsible for my frown?" she pointed out. "I came here expecting peace, not hassles."

"And as I pointed out last night, I expected someone Agnes' age, not a snip of a girl who looks about thirteen right now as you do."

Sara felt suddenly self-conscious as she remembered that she had not bothered with makeup earlier. But then, how in the world could she have expected a visitor so early in the morning? She felt at a decided disadvantage and it irritated her. "I assure you, I'm quite grown up and I can even manage to look sophisticated when the occasion demands it."

"Is that so?" he asked with a devilish twinkle in his eyes. "That's a transformation I'd like to see sometime. Though I think I'd still probably prefer the way you looked last night in your nightgown and robe. Very cuddly."

Sara was not amused. Her voice came cold and abrupt. "I distinctly remember you telling me I was far too skinny. But frankly, I'd just as soon we dropped this discussion. I really don't much care what you think of my looks. Or of me, period."

"I see." A shuttered expression came down over his eyes. "Well, I suppose I'd better be on my way. Good day, Miss Scott." He turned and strode quickly toward his truck.

Sara stared at his back with mingled aggravation

and consternation. *Let him go,* her rational mind told her. But her conscience pushed her forward, and with slow footsteps she followed behind him.

"Mr. Farrell?"

Doug's hand was on the door handle when he swung around, obviously surprised to discover her standing just behind him.

"Yes?" His voice was clipped and impatience flickered across his face.

"I—" Sara lowered her gaze to the ground so she could avoid the piercing intensity of his eyes. "I haven't thanked you yet for the firewood. I really do appreciate your thoughtfulness."

"You're very welcome," he answered in a slightly thawing tone.

Sara braved herself to look at him after all. "The least I can do to repay you for your trouble is to offer you a cup of coffee. If you have time?" she asked hesitantly. "I've got some already made."

Doug smiled abruptly, dispelling his harsh reserve and Sara caught her breath at his magnetism. She had forgotten just how compelling he could be.

"Thanks," he accepted easily. "I'd appreciate that."

On their way toward the back of the cabin, Doug paused beside the woodpile, scooped several logs into his arms and said, "Might as well carry in enough to start you off tonight. Just hold the door open for me, will you?"

While Doug carried the logs into the living room, Sara turned the burner on beneath the coffee pot and pulled out another cup and saucer from the cupboard. As she placed it on the table, her stomach rumbled hungrily.

When Doug came back into the room she said over her shoulder, "This mountain air seems to be doing something to my appetite. I'm going to make breakfast. Would you like to share it with me?"

"Sounds fine if you'll let me help," he replied. "I'm hungry myself."

Sara started the sausage frying in a skillet while Doug set the table and rescued the coffee from the stove before it boiled. Then Sara took a carton of eggs from the refrigerator, extracted one egg with her right hand, attempted to break it on the edge of a bowl. It was her injured hand and it still lacked strength. The egg shell only barely tapped against the bowl, not even hard enough to crack it.

She bit her lower lip in frustration, tried again and failed. Just at that moment his darkly tanned hand took the egg from her resistless fingers. "Let me," Doug said quietly.

"Thanks." Sara was too embarrassed even to look at him and she moved quickly to the stove where she picked up a fork with her left hand and began awkwardly turning the sausage.

"What happened to you?" Doug asked in a matter-of-fact voice as he broke several eggs into the bowl.

Sara sighed. "I was in an accident."

"I'm sorry," he said, sounding as though he genuinely meant it. "So Agnes wasn't putting me on about her friend needing a place to recuperate?"

"No," Sara answered briefly. "She wasn't."

"Will your leg and hand be all right in time?"

"So the doctors tell me. Some days I believe them, some days not."

"And one of the 'not' times is when you can't do something simple like break an egg, hmm?"

"Exactly."

"Well, I wouldn't let it get me down if I were you. I'm sure with enough practice you'll soon be able to break enough eggs to make a pound cake."

Sara looked up at him suspiciously, but there was not a trace of sarcasm on his face. His eyes met hers in a steady regard and there was only friendliness and encouragement in them. He flashed her a quick smile, which Sara found herself returning.

But as they sat down to eat she sternly reminded herself to remember the past. She must not be lulled by Doug's amiable attitude so that she forgot even for a single instant. At all costs, she must keep up her guard.

She forgot, remembered and forgot again at least a dozen times during the meal. Doug asked personal questions in a casually curious way, the way strangers do when they are getting acquainted and Sara concocted entirely fabricated answers. When he asked what she had done prior to her accident, she told him she had been a clerk in a dress shop in Los Angeles. When he seemed surprised that Agnes would have been on close terms with her, she feigned indignation that he seemed to find Agnes a cut above such an ordinary person. It threw Doug on the defensive as his face showed his annoyance.

"I wasn't implying any such thing," he grated out. "It's just that Agnes is a very busy woman and I had assumed most of her friends would be people in the entertainment business."

Like Sheila Starr, Sara told herself and she wondered whether Doug even remembered her at all. She had been worrying about the possibility of his recognizing her when he had told her she seemed familiar last night. But Sara wondered if it was actually a form of conceit that she had assumed that even if she still looked the same, still went by that name, he would have known her. Three years ago he had shown her very clearly how unimportant she was to him. So on what basis, really, could she conclude that he would have still known her if she had not changed? True, her stage name was now a famous one, but not all of the population listened to pop music and certainly she could not visualize Doug as being the type of man who read the TV or movie gossip columns. It could just be that he had never even heard the name Sheila Starr since he had left her that night and that she had since completely escaped his mind.

For some reason, it was a depressing thought and to hide her sudden unhappiness, Sara stood up, went to the stove and lifted the coffee pot. "Would you like a refill?" she asked with her back still turned to him.

"Maybe just half a cup," he agreed.

Sara gripped the handle as tightly as she could with her right hand and carried the coffee pot to the table and carefully poured the hot liquid into first Doug's cup and then her own. Once or twice the coffee pot wobbled and though she could feel his eyes upon her, this time he did not offer to help.

When she sat down again, he said, "Tell me, why did you come here alone? Don't you have any family who should be taking care of you back in California?"

Sara shook her head. "No."

"Not even a boyfriend?"

Sara thought of Pete, and of the dozens of men who had flattered and pursued her the past few years. Last of all, she thought once more of Doug himself, the only man she had ever loved, and how it had ended between them and her face grew bitter. "No, Doug, not even a boyfriend."

His sudden stillness alerted her that something was wrong. "How did you know my name?" he asked abruptly. "I'm sure I didn't mention it last night."

Sara froze and her heart pounded in her throat. *Idiot!* she jeered at herself silently. Doug's probing questions had dug beneath her defenses and now look what a colossal slipup she had made! Frantically, she searched her brain for an explanation that would sound reasonable.

Like a miracle, it came. "Agnes mentioned your name. She told me you were my landlord and that I would probably meet you."

Doug nodded, apparently satisfied with her answer. "And I know your name from the lease agreement you signed." He grinned suddenly. "We might as well be on a first name basis as not, now that we've broken bread together." He pushed back his chair and stood up. "Thanks for the breakfast, Sara. Be seeing you."

After Doug left, Sara spent the remainder of the morning settling in. Agnes had made sure that the cabin was well stocked with not only groceries and dishes, but other needed household supplies such as bed linens and bath towels. Besides the piano and stereo, she had also shipped several box loads of Sara's personal things, clothes, books, pictures and the like and those had yet to be unpacked. Included was a color photo of Pete, which she placed on prominent display on the bedroom dresser.

At noon, she called it quits. She ate a sandwich for lunch and then could no longer resist the lure of the outdoors. Now that the day had warmed up, she shed her sweater in favor of a short-sleeved shirt and set out downhill toward the creek once again. The entire time she had been unpacking, she had been fighting a battle with herself because she had wanted to rush outside into the sunlight and feel the freedom of the outdoors again.

She poked along the creek, following its twisting, westerly direction. In places, the forest grew thick along the bank, casting dark, mysterious shadows over the water. Boulders and smaller stones of all shapes and sizes littered the shallow rushing stream and after a time Sara sat down on one large, flat-topped rock and leaning forward, dabbled her hand in the icy water. Sunlight broke through the dark penetration of shadows, warming her body if not the water.

She wished suddenly that Pete could have been here with her to enjoy such a pleasant, secluded spot. Then she thought with stunned surprise, *Why, he would have hated it!* And the thought sliced through her with sharp razor-edged pain. Pete most definitely would not have liked it. Oh, he might have said, "It's pretty," and then left it without a backward glance or a further thought. Pete had been a city person. He liked being around swarms of people, going to exciting places, doing exciting things. Parties, night clubs, shows—those were the things he loved and thrived on. He had even told her once that he got all the solitude he needed whenever he was busy composing a song. After that he needed bright lights and people, not softly gurgling streams in a quiet mountain forest. The realization made him seem farther away than ever now, more unreachable even than at his death.

But a man who did share her enthusiasm for the beauty of the mountains was Doug. The thought came unbidden and unwelcomed as well, but nevertheless, it was true. When she had known him in Los Angeles, he had spoken of the Rockies in glowing terms and now she reluctantly conceded to herself that it had been his description that had caused her to want to see and experience them for herself. True, it had been Pete's idea to have a skiing holiday in Aspen with a group of their friends, but it had been her own idea to find an isolated mountain cabin to live in after her long hospitalization.

Yet, how could she possibly have guessed that Agnes would lease a cabin for her from Doug? She had never told Agnes about meeting him at her party, or of falling in love with him, and she had certainly not known he even owned a cabin. He had told her he owned a business in Denver, but there had been nothing in that statement to lead her to connect him with a cabin fifty miles away. No, it was just sheer bad luck that she should meet him again, and now she wondered what she should do. The beauty and peace of this place was exactly what she wanted for awhile, until she grew totally fit again and could decide what to do with the rest of her life. But despite his friendliness this morning, Doug didn't want her here and after the near fiasco when she had absent-mindedly said his name, she wasn't sure it was wise to remain. What if sometime she should really give herself away?

She shuddered and, with all the willpower she possessed, thrust the disturbing thought away. At least she needn't leave immediately. Surely she would not see him again in the very near future and she might as well enjoy herself for a few days before she made a definite decision about what to do next.

Perhaps, she thought now as she got to her feet and moved slowly upstream, there were other cabins for lease in this same general area. It was a possibility worth checking into and if there was one, she could still spend her months in the mountains without the danger of running into Doug.

Cheered by that idea, she picked up a large stick and began working her way up the tree-shrouded slope.

A half hour later she was nearing the top of a rise. From a distance she could hear a shout of child-like laughter. There must be a family living nearby, she thought in surprise.

When she reached the top and broke free of the trees, she was looking across a grassy plateau. Several yards away were a man and a boy. The boy, who looked to be about eleven or twelve, was in a wheelchair and the man was tossing a volley ball toward him. The boy caught it, threw it back and the man missed it. The boy laughed again as the man turned to fetch the still rolling ball.

The ball came to rest at Sara's feet. Impulsively, she stooped to pick it up and when she was upright once again, the man was only a foot or so away from her.

"Good afternoon," he greeted in the friendliest of voices. "Are you a lost hiker?"

Sara smiled in answer to his question and shook her head. "No. At least I hope I'm not lost. I've leased a cabin somewhere over there," she waved a hand vaguely in the direction she thought was the cabin's and added, "I was just out for a walk."

"Ah, we're neighbors, then. I'm Vernon West," he said as he held out a hand toward her.

"I'm Sara Scott." Sara shook hands with him and then she became aware that the boy in the wheelchair had come to join them.

"Billy, this is Miss Scott," Vernon West introduced them. "She says she's leased a cabin nearby."

"Hello," Billy said politely. "Want to play ball with us?"

Before Sara could answer, the man said, "I have a better idea. Why don't we invite her to come back to the house with us and meet Kate and the others?"

"Kate?"

"My wife," Vernon replied. He had clear gray eyes and now the eyes were frankly assessing as he looked at her. "You look as though you could use a calorie or two," he said kindly, "and my wife is just the one to give them to you with a large hunk of her chocolate cake."

"You tempt me very much," Sara laughed, "but perhaps your wife is busy and wouldn't exactly care to be interrupted just now."

"Nonsense," Vernon West answered. "Sometimes it gets a bit lonely out here. She'd love to meet you."

"Sure, she would," Billy seconded. "Kate loves company. Come on." Expertly, he turned his wheelchair about and began moving away from them. But a yard or two away, he stopped and turned to see whether the other two were coming or not.

Vernon West gave Sara a quizzical look and she laughed, shrugged her shoulders and moved toward Billy. "Why not?" she said. "I never could resist chocolate cake."

Billy frowned as he noticed her limp. "What happened to you?" he asked bluntly as Sara and the man began walking along on each side of the wheelchair.

"I was in an accident," she replied calmly.

"Really? So was I. That's why I'm in this thing." He indicated the wheelchair with a wave of his hand.

"I'm sorry," Sara said honestly.

Billy shrugged his thin shoulders. "Oh, it's not always so bad. When I'm in the house or on a cement surface I can beat Mr. Elton in a race."

"Who's Mr. Elton?" Sara asked curiously as she struggled to keep apace with the swiftly moving chair.

"He's my teacher. You'll probably get to meet him if he's still at the house flirting with Miss Gilly."

"And who is Miss Gilly?" Sara asked as she tried not to laugh.

"She's the physical therapist who comes three times a week to put me on the torture rack."

Now Sara openly grinned. "Ah—a heartless monster," she said, nodding. "I knew a few of those myself while I was in the hospital. They get a lot of pleasure out of making other people's lives miserable."

"That's the truth!" Billy said vehemently. "Of

course," he conceded after a moment's reflection, "she *can* be nice sometimes, like when she took me to the circus. And she's pretty, too. I guess that's why Mr. Elton likes to kiss her when he thinks nobody's looking."

"Billy!" Vernon West's voice was sharp. "Have you been spying again? Shame on you!"

Billy grinned unrepentantly. "Didn't have to. They were right there in the hallway the other day when I came out of the kitchen."

"I hope you were polite enough to leave before they could see you."

"Nope. I stayed to watch and they sure did look silly being so mushy. Vern, is kissing *really* fun?" He asked with a note of incredulity in his voice.

Sara and the man both laughed aloud and then Vernon tousled Billy's sandy-topped head and winked at Sara. "That's for grown-ups to know and for you to find out yourself someday, young man."

They had crossed the long grassy area and were now on a manicured back lawn behind a large white two-storied house. There was a swimming pool to one side of the yard surrounded by a patio and off in the distance was a barn and a fenced field where several horses were grazing.

Vernon led Sara into a roomy pine-trimmed kitchen where he introduced her to three people who were there, his wife Kate and the spied upon couple, Wayne Elton and Beth Gilly.

"You're going to be our neighbor?" Kate asked with a delighted smile as she shook Sara's hand. "That's grand. Have a seat and I'll pour you a cup of coffee. Or would you rather have iced tea?"

"I promised Sara a slice of your cake, honey," Vernon said, "or has Wayne already polished it off?"

"Well, he *did* have two helpings," Kate said with a distinct twinkle in her hazel eyes, "but there's still some left. I threatened him with my rolling pin if he dared to try for a third."

"So he snitched some of mine instead," Beth said.

"Hey, no fair!" Wayne complained. "Everybody's ganging up on me here. Billy, aren't you going to stick up for me?"

Billy grinned and shook his head. "No, Sir. A kid's not expected to stick up for his *teacher!*"

Wayne scowled at him. "I'll teach you to have respect for your tutor," he growled threateningly. "Just wait till I load you down with an English essay assignment tomorrow."

"Ugh! I'm getting out of here!" Billy, with a disgusted expression on his face, turned his chair quickly and wheeled out of the room, ignoring the burst of laughter behind him.

Over the next half hour, Sara got acquainted with the others and realized that she was really enjoying herself. Kate was slender and almost as tall as her husband, though she appeared to be several years younger than he, and the easy way they spoke to one another indicated that they shared a close and warm relationship. Wayne Elton was probably in his late twenties, a nice-looking young man with thick blond hair, laughing green eyes and an obviously well-developed sense of humor. Beth Gilly, as Billy had mentioned, was very pretty indeed. She had long brown hair, which curled and waved saucily about her face, and her eyes were an unusual and lovely shade of pale blue.

"You have a beautiful home here, Mrs. West," Sara said when Kate placed a slice of cake in front of her.

Kate laughed and shook her head as she sat down across the table from Sara. "I'm Kate," she said firmly, "and this isn't our house. We just work here."

"Oh, I see." Sara felt a twinge of embarrassment over her perfectly natural mistake.

"Vern and I came almost four years ago," Kate explained. "When Vern's friend, J.D., took on the care of Billy." Her face softened. "Billy lost his mother when he was just a little baby and then he lost his father too, in a car wreck. The accident left him crippled. J.D. and Billy's father were close friends and when no relatives came forward to claim him, J.D. petitioned the court to be named Billy's legal guardian."

"Your employer sounds like a very kind person," Sara murmured.

Vernon nodded as he draped an arm around his wife's shoulder. "He is," he agreed. "At the time it all happened, we had just lost a baby ourselves. When J.D. took Billy, he needed someone to be here with him all the time, of course, and he thought taking care of a child who really needed her would help Kate out of her depression, which it did." He smiled fondly at his wife.

Kate smiled back. "It's worked out perfectly for Vern as well," she said softly. "He loves to work outdoors and he hated the job he had before we came. Now he keeps up the grounds, the cars and takes care of the horses. We're saving money to buy a piece of land for our own home in the near future."

"That's if J.D. ever finds himself a wife or another housekeeper who can do as good a job with Billy as Kate," Beth laughingly informed Sara. "She's not about to ever move out and leave him unless she's satisfied with her replacement."

"That's true," Kate admitted, "but I might be willing if it were you who took over for me. Billy thinks you're pretty special."

"Only when I'm not making him do his exercises," Beth said ruefully.

"Well, if it's a wife J.D. is looking for, he'll just

have to look in another direction," Wayne growled. "I may have some plans of my own for your future."

Beth blushed charmingly, glanced at her watch and stood up. "Well, right now my future plans include a therapy session with Billy if I'm to earn my salary." She smiled at Sara. "It was nice meeting you. I hope to see you again soon."

A few minutes later, Sara left and made her way back to her cabin along the winding road this time. The going was easier on her leg because it was a downhill trek. But after she had walked the mile or so and arrived home, her leg was aching a good deal and she was glad to take a hot bath and rest for awhile.

She had enjoyed her visit with the neighbors. Kate and Vernon had warmly pressed her to visit them again soon and Wayne Elton and Beth Gilly had also been very friendly. Sara had gone home with the happy feeling that she had made some genuine new friends.

During the night it stormed, and for the next three days the cold and rain and even sleet were reminiscent of winter. Sara's spirits sank into gloom. She couldn't take any rambling walks and since she had yet to drive the car on these rocky, steep roads, she decided stormy weather was not the time to begin. Before the accident, though she had appreciated the beauty of nature, she had never been addicted to it. But now she could easily understand how people who had been in prison found it difficult to stay inside four walls once they were freed. It was exactly the way she felt after those long months of confinement in the hospital and she yearned for the weather to clear so that she could be outdoors again.

The long, wet days hung heavy on her hands and she often wandered from room to room like a lost soul, and reluctantly came to the conclusion that

Agnes had been right. She should have gone back to L.A. and made an effort to resume her life there. This isolated place was a mistake and depression settled over her like a thick layer of winter snow on a mountain top.

On the third evening, the rain still came down in torrents. A long, dull evening stretched ahead. The TV was out. The storm had taken care of that and Sara was tired of reading and heartily sick of her own thoughts. For the first time, she approached the piano. With her weak hand, she doubted if she could play, but she sat down anyway and lifted the lid.

She picked out a few notes with her left hand and then after a moment, she tried the right hand. She had trouble stretching her fingers out to reach some of the keys and a few times she hit the wrong notes, but she kept trying, stopping to rest and then trying again.

After a while, almost unconsciously, she began playing one of Pete's compositions, which had been one of her more successful recordings, and soon she was singing the words. Her voice was rusty, but gradually the tones became more clear, more bell-like as the sound echoed around the room.

The unexpected sound of someone pounding on the front door startled her and her hands crashed down heavily on the keys, creating a harsh, discordant noise. Sara got to her feet, wondering why anyone would be out on such an evening.

When she opened the door, she found Doug Farrell standing there. Rivulets of rain fell from his bare head down onto his face and onto his tan raincoat. Sara stared at him blankly for a moment, until he said, "It's sort of wet out here. Do you mind if I come in?"

"Of course not." She moved back a pace so that he could enter.

He walked across the room to stand dripping in front of the flames that were blazing in the fireplace. "It's rotten weather out tonight," he murmured.

"It certainly is," she agreed. Her eyes were puzzled as she looked at him. "Surely these mountain roads are too dangerous to drive right now. Was it really necessary for you to come here tonight?"

"It was." But instead of elaborating at once, he glanced curiously around the room. "I thought I heard voices in here before I knocked."

Sara's lips twisted into a derisive smile. "The noisy party?" She shrugged her shoulders. "Search the place if you like. You'll find no one here but me."

Doug's gaze swung back to her face and there was a glint of anger in his eyes. "That wasn't what I meant at all and you know it. But I *did* hear music and voices."

"One voice," she corrected coldly. "I was playing the piano and singing. Is that against the rules, too?"

With the swiftness of a mountain lion, Doug crossed the room and grabbed Sara's arms in a punishing grip and gave her a little shake. "I did not get out in this storm tonight simply to come here and listen to your sarcastic barbs," he grated out.

"Then why did you come?" Sara jerked herself free from his bruising hands and began rubbing her arms tenderly. "Surely this isn't just a social call."

"I came to warn you that the bridge down the hill is washed out. I was afraid you might try to go that way tomorrow or in the near future."

"Thank you very much," Sara said stiffly, "but you could have telephoned and saved yourself a trip."

"No, I couldn't," he contradicted. "I tried to call, but your line is out. And because it is, I want you to pack a bag. You're coming home with me until the weather clears."

45

"Don't be ridiculous!" Sara snapped. "I don't intend to go anyplace tonight and most certainly not with you!"

Doug's eyes narrowed into dark slits. "I'd like to throttle you," he told her in a grim voice. "I don't believe I've ever met a more obstinate, pigheaded girl in my life!" He signed heavily. "Look, I have a live-in housekeeper, so you'll be well chaperoned if it's your virtue you're concerned about."

"I'm not," Sara denied bitterly. "I can't imagine myself being the type to appeal to *you*, but all the same, I see no reason to leave here. I'm perfectly content."

It was a bald-faced lie, of course, but Sara would have died before admitting to Doug that she was already lonely, not to mention slightly frightened at the intensity of the flood that seemed to have no end.

"Your feelings don't enter into this," Doug said with annoyance. "A bridge is washed out. You're on high ground here, but even you must have glanced out your window and seen how swollen Lucky Creek is. Your telephone is dead and you're unfamiliar with these roads even in the best weather. What if you get sick or hurt? There would be no way you could summon help. All I'm suggesting is that you stay a few days at my house until the weather clears up, the waters recede and your telephone is back in service. I don't want to be worrying about your being here alone."

"Then don't! When did I ask you to worry about me? I'll manage just fine, thank you. All I want from you is to be left alone!"

Doug's mouth pressed into a harsh line and his jaw resembled stone. Angrily, he nodded before striding to the door. "I'll be happy to oblige you, then. The last thing I need in my home is a quarrelsome guest." He paused and glanced back at her assessingly, and even before he spoke again, Sara could tell it was a very low assessment. "I wonder why Agnes chose to be friends with someone like you." He gave his head a shake and opened the door. *"She* doesn't have a warped personality."

Chapter Three

Doug's cutting words still had the power to both hurt and anger Sara four days later. *Warped personality!* The words rankled and made her want to lash out at him, to retaliate, to hurt him back the way he had hurt her. She sputtered and raged to herself as she remained isolated those days in the cabin, and her loneliness increased with each passing day. The rains had finally stopped, but the grounds were so water-logged there was no point in attempting to take a walk. And the roads were so muddy she would have been terrified of skidding right off the side of the mountain if she had dared to venture out in the car. The telephone remained dead and she felt as though she was cut off from the entire world.

Which is only your own fault, she told herself in all fairness, whenever the rage at Doug abated enough for her conscience to give him due credit. He *had* invited her to stay in his home. If she had only swallowed her pride and gone she would at least have had the company of his housekeeper during these past dreary days. But the fact remained that she had not and since then Doug had quite pointedly left her to herself.

She found herself wondering where Doug lived. Denver, she supposed, since that was where his business was located. Probably he had built this cabin as a get-away weekend place and then finding that he didn't use it often enough to justify having it, had decided to lease it.

But not to a single woman, she reminded herself tartly, whipping up the dying embers of anger against him once again. And all at once the word "single" made her realize that she had no way of knowing whether he was married or not himself. She had assumed, when they had met the first time, that he was not, but now—three years later?

The idea was disturbing and her mind refused to let go of the question. When he had insisted she stay in his house, he had only mentioned a housekeeper, not a wife. But what did that prove?

Now Sara was angry with herself. Why should it matter to her one way or another if Doug should have a wife and a dozen children? He was nothing in her life. He never had been, actually. He had only been a brief interlude that she should have forgotten entirely by now.

The following morning she awoke to find the day brilliantly flooded with golden sunlight and when she stepped outside she found that the ground had dried considerably. Her spirits soared at the magnificence of the beauty that met her eyes, and once more she was delighted that she was here in this spot in the mountains. Forgotten were the past few miserable days and her anger at Doug as she rushed back indoors to make her breakfast and afterward, to bake a batch of brownies.

In midafternoon, she set out on foot toward the big house. She took the road instead of the woods, knowing it would make the uphill walk easier and smoother. In the crook of one arm, she carried a cardboard box filled with brownies.

One good thing about the sedentary life she was living was that she had ample time to sharpen her cooking skills. It was a hobby she had always been interested in but had never had much opportunity to practice. The only problem was that she had no one to share the results with, except now, when she could carry a little offering to Billy.

She smiled reminiscently as she thought of the few meals she had prepared for Pete. He had teased her that she was a hopelessly frustrated housewife and, in truth, he had been right. She had loved her singing and, of course, had enjoyed her success, but she had always hated the publicity and constant travel. Her greatest delight and relaxation had been to return to her apartment, which she was constantly decorating and redecorating, and clean it herself and cook her own meals. Maybe, she mused now, that was what she was really cut out for in life—the role of wife, mother and homemaker. Unfortunately, such a prospect did not appear to loom on her horizon.

Shrugging off the thought, Sara let herself enjoy the moment. She inhaled the fresh air deeply, savoring its clean pine scent. A light wind whispered through the trees that bordered the road. Once there was a break in the thick stand and she looked straight down a steep precipice. Probably a snow avalance at one time had mowed down this particular stand of forest, leaving this odd, ugly gape down the mountainside.

Majestic spruces and pines shielded the large house from the road, so that its privacy was inviolate and as Sara moved slowly up the drive she was impressed once again at what a beautiful house it was. It had a welcoming, warm quality about it rather than the cold, austere beauty of many estate-type homes. She couldn't help but think how wonderful it would be to live in such a house with one's own husband and family.

She shook her head impatiently. What was wrong with her today, she wondered. She seemed to be hung up on the idea of marriage. Maybe all those lonely days in the cabin had addled her brain.

A blue station wagon was parked in front of the house and seeing it, Sara paused and bit her lip in consternation. She had looked forward to a visit with Kate and Billy and the others. But she didn't want to intrude if they had visitors. Still, she did have the brownies for Billy and it would be a shame to go away again without leaving them for him.

After a moment's hesitation, she mounted the wide, rounded front terrace and pressed the doorbell. She would just leave the box and go on her way.

Vernon opened the heavy, carved door and smiled when he saw her. "Well, Sara, how did you fare through the storm? Kate tried to call you several times, but your line was out."

Sara grimaced. "It still is or I would have called before coming today."

"That doesn't matter in the least," Vernon said. "Come on in."

Sara shook her head. "No, I see," she said, waving her hand toward the car behind her, "that you already have a guest, so I won't stay." She held out the box toward him. "I baked a little something for Billy and the rest of you, so I'll just leave it and—"

"Nonsense." Vernon put his hand on her elbow and guided her into the house. "Kate'll be happy to see you."

Almost before she realized it, Sara was inside the living room, a huge room done in cinnamon and burnt orange colors, which gave it a warm, cozy look despite its vast size. A stone fireplace dominated the wall at the opposite end of the room. Kate sat on the sofa, chatting with a man who was in a nearby chair.

"Look who's here, Kate," Vernon announced from behind Sara's left shoulder.

Kate glanced up and then rose. "How nice to see you again, Sara," she said with a quick smile. "Come meet a friend of ours, Dr. Royce Carpenter. Royce, this is Sara Scott, a new neighbor of ours."

The doctor had risen to his feet also and now he came forward and shook hands with Sara. He was a silvery-haired man in his early fifties, Sara gauged, and the skin crinkled around his hazel eyes as he smiled. "I'm pleased to meet you, Miss Scott," he said.

"Thank you, Doctor," Sara said, smiling back. Now she added apologetically, "I saw your car outside and I told Vernon I didn't want to intrude. I just brought something by for Billy."

"Brownies," Vernon explained succinctly.

"Hmmph. One more person around to spoil that boy," the doctor said disapprovingly.

"Ha! You're a fine one to talk!" Kate exclaimed. "Know why the doctor stopped by today?" she asked Sara, and without waiting for a reply, answered her own question. "He came to give Billy a collie pup!"

Sara laughed while the doctor had the grace to look shamefaced and made an attempt to extract a promise from Kate to keep quiet to J.D. about how Billy got the puppy. Kate refused, vowing instead to lay the blame squarely where it belonged and vowing further to telephone the doctor in the wee hours of the night when the dog's yapping made her own sleep impossible.

At last the teasing ended and Kate and Vernon went away, Kate to get refreshments, Vernon to check on Billy and his puppy.

"Are you Billy's doctor?" Sara asked as the two of them, being left alone, sat down on the sofa.

Dr. Carpenter nodded. "At times. I'm the one who takes care of the routine things like chicken pox and colds, but he sees a specialist about the condition of his legs. I'm a friend of his guardian."

"Will Billy ever walk again?" Sara couldn't help asking.

"I can't say," the doctor replied. "It's doubtful, but on the other hand, he can get around on crutches now and they never even expected that much mobility in the beginning."

"I guess there's at least a small measure of hope or else they wouldn't keep up with the physical therapy?"

"Right. There's always hope and sometimes miracles have been known to happen. I've seen enough in my time to never completely rule out any possibility." Dr. Carpenter's keen eyes met Sara's. "You've had a bit of trouble with your own legs," he stated matter-of-factly. "You were limping when you came in."

Sara nodded. "Like Billy, I was in an accident too, but I never lost complete use of my limbs. Actually, the worst injuries were internal and then my face. I underwent several operations in addition to extensive plastic surgery. I only left the hospital recently after a stay of several months."

"I see. I imagine you're heartily sick of doctors then, aren't you?"

"Yes," Sara agreed instantly. "Just the thought of them makes me—oh!" She clasped a hand over her lips and blushed as she realized what she was saying. "Forgive me, Doctor— I didn't mean to be rude!"

The doctor threw back his head and laughed with genuine amusement. "It's all right," he told her with a chuckle. "If I'd been in your position I imagine I'd feel the same way. But I do hope your aversion to us as a group of professionals doesn't extend to us on a social basis?"

"Of course not, Dr. Carpenter," she quickly reassured him.

"Royce," he corrected with a little grin. "We're going to be friends."

Sara laughed and nodded. "In that case, call me Sara."

Just then, Kate reappeared bearing a tray laden with coffee and a plate of Sara's brownies. Following her were Vernon, Billy and the new puppy. Billy wheeled his chair to Sara's side so that she could examine his new friend and she duly admired the squirming little ball of tan fur.

"What's his name?" she asked.

"I haven't decided yet," Billy replied. "It ought to be a strong sounding name, 'cause he's gonna grow up to be big and strong. Maybe Duke or Tiger," he mused. "What do you think, Sara?"

"Those are nice names," she conceded, "but how about Rocky?"

"Rocky?"

She nodded. "For the mountains. They are certainly strong enough."

"I like that," Billy said with a nod. "Rocky. What do you think, Doc?"

"Sounds great to me," Royce told him. He glanced at his watch and got to his feet, saying regretfully, "I'm afraid I don't have time for the coffee, Kate. I've got an appointment to keep." He looked at Sara and added, "It was nice meeting you. I hope to see you again."

Sara stayed on for awhile after the doctor left. Kate, it seemed, was as eager for company after the enforced isolation from the rains as Sara had been. Because the weather had been so bad, neither Billy's tutor nor physical therapist had arrived during the past few days, though both were due to come again the following day. The two women got to know one another better while Vernon and Billy went outside with the puppy. Before Sara decided it was time to leave, Kate had invited her to return the following Saturday as a guest for Billy's birthday party.

There were a couple of hours of daylight left when Sara departed, but she was still far from ready to return to her cabin. When she reached the road, she decided to continue walking further uphill. Late afternoon shadows from the trees cast cool dark splotches across the road as she climbed, but she paid no attention to the swiftly cooling air as she once again felt the exhilaration of being out in the open.

An hour later she came to the crest of the hill and had a magnificent view of towering mountain ranges in the distance. As she paused to drink in its splendor she shivered and for the first time became aware of the sharp chill in the air. She had walked a long way and now she had yet to return. If she didn't start now, and hurry at that, darkness would catch her. The thought made her nervous. Out here in this rugged countryside there were no such things as streetlamps to guide one's way.

The return downhill was naturally speedier than the uphill jaunt had been, but still the shadows grew thicker, darker and more chilling and Sara was acutely conscious of a throbbing in her bad leg. She had pushed it to the limit today in her eagerness to be outdoors again and now it was more painful than ever. Her gait grew slower, her limp became more pronounced and each step became an agonizing ordeal.

When she passed the gate to the estate she had visited earlier, Sara longed to ask Vernon to drive her the remainder of the way home, but her pride refused to allow it. She had brought this pain upon herself by trying to do too much too soon and she was not going to impose on others now because of her own foolishness.

Darkness fell swiftly as she struggled onward. If there were a moon or stars this evening, Sara could catch no glimpse of them through the tree tops. The road was dark in the inky blackness and she stayed on it more by the feel of it beneath her feet than by sight.

She rounded a curve and, without warning, the blinding glare of headlights paralyzed her, pinning her against the edge of the narrow road. The car suddenly stopped with a loud squeal of tires only inches away from her even as she fell sideways toward the edge of the road.

A moment later she was attempting to sit upright when two strong arms came from out of the dark night to lift her into the air, and then she was carried to the car and placed inside it. The arms were infinitely gentle, but the stream of abusive words was a complete contradiction to the action.

"Of all the stupid, idiotic things to do!" The voice grumbled. "Don't you know better than to walk along the center of a mountain road at night? Do you even realize how close I came to running you down? If you want to commit suicide, at least use a method that doesn't involve innocent people!"

The interior overhead light in the car illuminated them both and Sara flinched beneath Doug's fiery gaze. She was now in a sitting position and the upper portion of his body was crouched over hers as he braced himself with his hands on either side of her. His face, so close to hers, was frightening with his intense anger.

Her words were stuck in her throat as the effects of the shock spread through her. "I . . . I'm sorry. . . ." she said weakly. She gave her head a little shake and stopped.

"Are you hurt?" Doug's voice was thick with anxiety now that his rage was fading.

Sara shook her head again. "No," she answered

thinly. "At least, I don't think so." Her eyes met his and with amazement, she saw now that he was trembling from his own reaction to shock. Without even stopping to think what she was doing, she lifted a hand and touched his face. "I'm all right, really," she whispered urgently. "Please, don't be upset."

"Don't?" Doug echoes incredulously. "Don't? When I think how close I came to killing you, I—" The words stopped, choked off by a shuddering emotion that vibrated through him. And then, swiftly, without warning, his arms were around her again, holding her tightly against his chest as his lips possessed hers.

It was a kiss that was all consuming, enveloping them both in the totality of its passion, holding them hostage beneath a power that was greater than either of their individual wills. Doug's mouth, hard, even ruthless in the beginning, softened with desire. Sara's lips parted beneath the infinite warmth and gentleness of his and a sigh of surrender escaped from her throat when they drew apart at last.

Doug was smiling at her and the tenderness in his eyes melted her bones even before he spoke, whispering, "You must have the softest, warmest lips in all the world. Who are you, really . . . a wood nymph come to practice your magic wiles on a hapless human?"

"And if I am?" she asked with a teasing smile.

"Then you must do your worst," he replied, laughing. "I'm entirely beneath your spell." His dark head bent low and he claimed her lips once more.

At last they returned to earth. Doug lifted his head and Sara's hand slid down from his shoulders. Reluctantly, he withdrew his arms from about her. "I'd better get you home," he said in a normal voice. "You say you're not hurt by your fall, but I want to be sure."

"It's nothing," she told him. "Just my leg. It's stiff from all the walking I did today."

"And which the fall can't have helped any," he said grimly. Doug backed out of the car, closed the passenger door and went around to slide beneath the steering wheel.

In only a few, short minutes, they had arrived at her cabin. When they got out of the car, Sara's leg buckled under her and once again, Doug scooped her up into his arms.

Inside the living room, Sara reached across his shoulder and flipped on the light switch. She thought then that he would put her down, but she was mistaken. Instead, he carried her across the room and entered her bedroom.

Once again, he paused by the door so that she could turn on the light and then at last he slowly released her. "What you need for that leg is a hot bath," he told her firmly. "I'll make something hot to drink." He turned toward the door, halted abruptly and turned back, grinning wickedly. "Unless you need my help here? Maybe even wood nymphs need—"

"Privacy," Sara stated positively, struggling not to laugh.

Doug sighed. "I was afraid you'd say that. All right, my lovely dryad, go splash in your water. But don't take too long or I'll have to come back to check on whether you really exist or are a figment of my imagination."

Sara smiled to herself as he left the room and almost dreamily, she prepared for her bath. She felt warm and happy all over, in spite of her stiff leg. Her lips quivered even now at the memory of his kiss.

Reality only returned after she was stretched out full-length in the bath. The heat of the water was penetrating her body, relaxing her muscles, but now her mind was no longer bemused or relaxed. What had happened earlier was sheer madness. This was Doug—the man who had hurt her so badly once before, yet here she was, bewitched by his compelling magnetism all over again. He had called her a wood nymph and accused her of putting him under a spell, but it was he who had put a magic hex on her! She had to put a stop to it, break the spell now, while she still could, or else it would be too late.

By the time she was dressed in a nightgown and her long, servicable robe and had walked out into the living room, she had completely regained her composure. A fire crackled invitingly in the stone fireplace and standing before it, gazing thoughtfully down into the flames, was Doug. He had shed his jacket and Sara's eyes dwelt on the breadth of his back and shoulders. Never had she been able to quite forget the smooth look of them, the feel of strength in them beneath her fingers. When he turned toward her, smiling, she quelled the memory and hardened her heart against the hypnotic pull of his gaze.

"I've warmed some soup for you and made some coffee," he said. "Come sit down and I'll serve you." He moved toward her and held out his hand to her. "I'm glad to see my wood nymph is real after all."

Instead of placing her hand in his, Sara held it up before her, as though to ward off his touch. "Please," she said softly, "no more of that. We . . . earlier tonight, we just sort of got carried away. We were both a bit in shock over the near accident and I think we'd better back off now."

Doug frowned. "Can we?" he asked. "There *was* a magic there between us . . . a chemistry, if you will. But whatever, it was there for both of us."

"Yes," Sara conceded honestly, since there was hardly any point in denying it. "There was, but it was a passion born of overwrought emotions. We don't even know each other and I have no intentions of being swept into something over my head just because of one brief interlude!"

For a moment she thought she had angered him, in a way, even hoped that she had. It would be easier if he were angry and affronted because then he would stay away and she wouldn't have to constantly keep up her defenses against him. But after a long silence while Doug's dark gaze studied her face, he finally nodded.

"Perhaps you're right," he said at last. "Things have moved a bit too fast. It's frightened you and frankly, I'm a bit leery of it, too. A long time ago I fell for a girl hard and fast, before we really had time to get acquainted. It was disastrous. I hurt her and ended up hating myself." His brows contracted over his eyes and suddenly he swept a hand across his face, as though banishing the picture his mind has just seen. Then he glanced at her again and smiled gently. "Come sit down and we'll just talk."

Somewhat to Sara's surprise, he kept his promise and for the next hour they sat before the fire just chatting amiably. Doug told her a couple of amusing stories about things that had happened to him and he soon had Sara relaxed and laughing. It was only when he asked questions about her own life that she became wary once again. She had lied to him before and now she must be careful not to slip and say something that might contradict it.

Even so, when he left, with just a friendly smile and a promise to get in touch with her soon, she had a pleasant feeling from the evening. Once again Doug had proven that he could be a fun and interesting companion. It was only on the personal, romantic level that she must be wary of him.

The following day Sara took the car and drove to Denver. There she bought a telescope for Billy's birthday gift, a new summer dress for herself and a few groceries to replenish her cupboards. When she got back home and entered the cabin, arms laden with packages, it was to the unexpected sound of the telephone ringing.

She deposited the bags on the kitchen table and rushed to pick up the receiver. Her heart beat erratically at the thought that it might be Doug.

Instead, it was an irate Agnes. "I've been trying to call you for three days!" she exclaimed. "Where have you been? I've been worried sick about you!"

"I've been here all along," Sara replied, "but a storm knocked the phone out of commission. I'm sorry you've been worried."

"Mmph. Well, as long as you're all right. You *are* all right, aren't you?"

Sara laughed. "Just fine, Mother Hen. How are you?"

"Busy. By the way, I just had a feeler from a record company about you yesterday. They're negotiating with Pete's parents on some of his compositions and they want you to record them."

"Not interested," Sara said firmly.

"Don't be silly," Agnes snapped. "The money—"

"Would be great," Sara answered for her, "but I don't want to do it, Agnes."

"Promise me you'll at least think it over," Agnes insisted. "In the meantime, I wonder if you'd like some company for a week or two?"

"You?" Sara asked. "I'd love it. When can you come?"

"Not for a couple of weeks. I've got quite a few loose ends to tie up first. I'll let you know when it's definite, but are you sure, Sara? I know you went up there to be alone and—"

"Not *that* alone! I just wanted to get away from that hospital and I wasn't ready to go back to L.A. Come as soon as you can."

The prospect of Agnes' visit eased the loneliness of the remainder of the day. Doug had been right—she was lonely. Even though the rains had stopped, even though she could now get out and about, she was still alone here. Her solitary meals were dreary and she had too much time to think about Pete's death, the end of her own career and about Doug himself. Last night she had lost control of her tightly bound emotions when he had kissed her, which only proved that she had never gotten him out of her system. If she didn't want to be hurt and humiliated by him again, she was going to have to be very careful.

She laughed at herself the next afternoon as she dressed in the new white and yellow sundress. Who would ever have thought Sheila Starr could be so eager to go to a twelve-year-old boy's birthday party? Agnes would shake her head in despair if she knew! But a party, any party, meant people, talk, companionship, and for a few hours at least, it would take her out of herself. One of these days soon she was going to have to seriously decide on a course for her future. She couldn't drift aimlessly forever. But for this afternoon, such considerations could be shelved.

The large living room had been transformed from its ordinary everyday appearance, Sara found when she entered it an hour later. Today balloons festooned the ceiling. Kate's crystal and ceramic knick-knacks had been removed from tables and in their places were dishes of nuts and candies.

The room was crowded with children as well as a few adults, and after briefly greeting the birthday boy himself, Sara turned to Vernon questioningly. "Since Billy has a tutor, somehow I never thought of him knowing a lot of children his own age. I had imagined him as being a lonely boy."

Vernon laughed and shook his head. "Not so. He

missed almost two years of school after the accident so that's why he needs Wayne to help him catch up, which he's just about done. In the fall, he'll go to regular school in Lucky. These youngsters are his classmates there. Even though Billy hasn't attended classes on a daily basis, he's visited the school a few times and the kids have been out here for picnics and weiner roasts. Billy's definitely a part of the pack. He's just as ornery as any other boy his age. See?"

Billy had taken a balloon, stretched it thin, then shot it at another boy, popping him in the shoulder. The other boy retaliated by blowing a whistle in Billy's face. Then the two boys began wrestling with their hands, both shouting with laughter.

"I see," Sara laughed.

"Come across the room and I'll introduce you to the grown-ups." Vernon took her elbow in his hand and guided her through the wriggling throng of youngsters.

"You've met Doc, of course," Vernon reminded as they reached a spot near the fireplace.

"It's nice to see you again, Sara," Royce Carpenter said as she offered him her hand.

"It's nice to see you again, too," she responded with a quick smile.

Vernon pressed her elbow and guided her away. "I want to introduce you to J.D., Sara," he added.

Sara looked up to meet two amused, dark eyes and she gasped with surprise. Doug looked very elegant in a cream-colored suit with a dark brown shirt. The jacket was tailored to fit his broad shoulders to perfection. Today he looked every inch the successful, wealthy businessman.

He lifted one eyebrow quizzically. "Coming to join our wild, noisy party, Miss Scott?"

Sara grinned wickedly. "Just that, Mr. Farrell. But I wouldn't think you would have the nerve to show your face!"

Doug chuckled, obviously enjoying the situation. "I wouldn't have if I'd known you were a guest."

Vernon looked from one to the other, beaming with pleasure. "You two already know each other?"

Doug nodded. "Miss Scott is leasing her cabin from me."

Vernon's mouth dropped open. "Well, I'll be darned. I didn't know it belonged to you, J.D." He turned to Sara. "We're glad you came, Sara, but if you'll excuse me, I'll leave you with J.D. now. I've got to help Kate with the refreshments and see how Wayne's coming along with the homemade ice cream."

When they were alone, Doug asked curiously, "How long have you known our little family here? Billy obviously likes you or you wouldn't have been invited today."

Sara shrugged. "Since about the second or third day I was here. They all mentioned J.D., but somehow I never connected him with my hostile landlord."

Doug grinned and his voice lowered so that no one could hear except her. "After the other night you can hardly call me hostile any longer, my little dryad." His gaze dwelt on her mouth.

Sara felt her face grow warm. "Stop it!" She ordered in a raspy voice. "This is hardly the place and—"

"Then later?" Doug asked quickly. "Tonight? I want very much to hold you in my arms again and—"

"No!" Panic surged through her. It was all just like before—Doug was giving her a rush, but it was purely physical attraction with him, nothing more! Her love for him had meant nothing to him then; if she allowed herself to get involved with him again, it could only end the same way. "No!" She repeated forcefully. "I'd prefer it if you'd just leave me alone. I'm really not in the market for a lighthearted affair."

There was a flicker of something that resembled pain in his deep midnight-black eyes and it surprised Sara as well as caused her a pang of regret. But she really could do nothing to alleviate it. Old memories had crowded in once more, hurting her too. In desperation, she quickly walked away from him, hardly aware of where she was going until she bumped into Wayne Elton, who stopped and spoke to her.

Somehow Sara got through the party with a smile, though all her former enthusiasm for it had vanished. To leave would be rude and would invite comments and speculations that she wished to avoid. It was fairly easy to remain carefully out of Doug's vicinity because he pointedly did not approach her. She helped Wayne and Beth set up the party games, laughed and joked with some of the children and joined in the singing of "Happy Birthday" when the cake, ablaze with candles, was carried in. She took pains, however, to sing in a low undertone so that her true carrying voice would not ring out. Things were bad enough already, finding out that Doug was "J.D.," the owner of this house, Billy's guardian and Vernon and Kate's employer. Now that he was so coldly furious with her, it would be a complete disaster if he should suddenly realize who she really was.

After Billy blew out the candles, Kate cut the cake and Beth and Sara served it, along with liberal portions of strawberry ice cream. With her own plate in hand, Sara joined Royce on the sofa.

"Are we crazy," Royce asked her with a smile, "or just young at heart, to be attending such a chaotic gathering as this?"

Sara giggled. "Probably a little bit of both." She

65

glanced at the children, all sitting on the floor in a large circle as they devoured their refreshments. Though their bodies were fairly still for now, the loud din of their chatter reverberated from the walls and ceiling. "It takes me back to my own childhood and the birthday parties I had." She shook her head. "They talk about the new generation, but some things don't seem to change at all."

There was a stir in the wide entrance to the room, and Sara, along with most of the others, glanced in that direction. Framed in the doorway was one of the most beautiful women she had ever seen, and in Los Angeles, she had seen many. This one had hair that was dark and wavy, a perfect foil for the milk whiteness of her skin. She wore an emerald green dress that hugged a perfect figure, which was slender yet curved in exactly the right places. Her vivid red lips were slightly parted and as Doug got up and went to greet her, she smiled and cried out, "Darling!" She held out both her hands as Doug neared her and then she leaned forward and kissed him fully on the lips.

A striking silence stilled the room as the children eyed the newcomer and Doug with frank curiosity. Then the woman finally drew back and with a little laugh, asked Doug, "Have I interrupted something?"

Doug's smile answered hers. "We're having a birthday party for Billy," he explained. "You're just in time for some cake and ice cream."

The dark-haired woman lifted her amused, perfectly arched eyebrows. "No thanks, darling," she refused, "but I could stand a drink."

"Of course," Doug said at once. He glanced up to see Kate nearby and beckoned her to join them. "Carla, you remember Kate, don't you? My housekeeper? Kate, how about introducing Carla to the others while I get her a drink?"

Kate did so, and a few minutes later Sara was introduced to Carla Bellamy, who at first exhibited a bored indifference as she greeted her.

"Are you a relative of one of the children, Miss Scott?"

"No." Kate answered for Sara. "She's a neighbor, a new friend of ours."

"A neighbor?" Carla frowned thoughtfully. "I had no idea Doug had any near neighbors."

Sara smiled. "Yes. I live in the cabin just down the hill, if you can call a mile or so 'near.'"

"You live there alone?" Carla probed.

All at once Sara disliked Carla Bellamy. There was something here she neither understood nor liked. Where before there had been a barely concealed tolerance of her on the other woman's part, now there was an insistent curiosity. Carla seemed to be studying Sara, as though assessing her competition. It seemed a ridiculous notion to Sara.

"Yes," she replied grudgingly. "I live there alone."

Carla shrugged her shoulders with a dismissive gesture. "It sounds boring," she stated emphatically. "And lonely." Then she turned to speak to Royce, whom it was soon apparent she already knew.

Royce politely stood up and shook hands with Carla Bellamy. "How've you been, Carla? Are you and your husband here paying a visit to your mother?"

Carla shook her head. "No," she replied. "I'm back for good. My husband and I were recently divorced."

"I'm sorry," Royce said gently.

"Oh, don't be!" Carla's laugh was light. "I'm not, I assure you! It's wonderful to be back home where I belong. Thank you, darling," she ended as Doug, reaching her side, handed her a drink.

The others drifted away and a little later, Sara

watched Doug and Carla talking animatedly near a window. It was as if the two of them were entirely alone, as though an invisible shield surrounded them, shutting out every other person in the room.

"Miss Bellamy and Doug must be very close friends," Sara observed to Royce. "They seem to have a great deal to talk about to each other."

Royce shrugged. "I'm not sure 'friends' is the correct word. Carla and J.D. were engaged until J.D. decided to take Billy into his home. Then she broke off with him, went away to Florida, I think it was, and married someone else."

"I see." Sara murmured softly. And she did—too clearly. When she had met Doug herself three years ago, it must have been shortly after Carla had left him. This new information supplied the missing puzzle pieces. It accounted for why he had been so hostile and cynical when she had mentioned her own love for him. Now Carla was back again.

Sara was furious over her own naivety and stupidity. When she had fallen in love with Doug, somehow the idea that he might be in love with another woman simply never occurred to her. Now she could see that his attentions to her had been the acts of a man desperate to forget someone else, but when she had come on seriously, it had angered and frightened him away.

At least Sara had the small comfort of knowing that her wary instincts against getting involved with him again had been true. It could only have led to renewed pain for her, because if any woman ever held the key to Doug's heart, it was most obviously Carla Bellamy—three years ago and today.

Chapter Four

Two days later Royce telephoned and invited Sara to dinner that same evening. "Sorry it's such short notice. I had originally intended to ask you for later in the week but meetings have eaten up every night except tonight. Are you insulted or will you take pity on a lonely bachelor?"

Sara laughed at his concern. "Tonight is fine," she said firmly. "I'll look forward to it."

"There's only one hitch," Royce said apologetically. "I may be a little late by the time I get away from the office and drive up for you."

"There's no need for you to come this far at all," Sara decided quickly. "I'll drive my car to Denver and meet you. It's too far for you to have to drive back and forth. You'd spend most of the evening on the road."

Royce chuckled. "I knew I liked you from the start and now I know why. It's because you're such a considerate girl, Sara. All right then, if you're sure you don't mind driving this far and back at night, why don't we plan to meet at my house around seven-thirty? We can have a drink before going to the restaurant."

"Just give me the directions," Sara replied, "and I'll be there."

That evening she bathed and then dressed in a

deceptively simple beige-toned dress. It was a de-
signer original that she had purchased last year and
after she slipped it on, Sara studied her image in the
mirror with a critical eye. The dress was still beautiful and of a timeless design. But she could not help
noticing that it was a little loose fitting at the hips
and waist and just a tiny bit too blousy at the
bustline.

Sara sighed as she viewed herself with displeasure.
She had put on a little weight the past couple of
weeks, but she was still painfully thin. And her hair
was hopeless! Little ringlets curled tightly against
her head and she hated them. Maybe it was stylish
these days, but it wasn't a style she liked for herself.
It seemed as though it would be forever before her
hair grew out to its normal shoulder length.

At least, she thought wryly as she lightly applied
some brown eye shadow and mascara, she was
beginning to grow used to her new face. A total
stranger no longer greeted her each time she happened to glance into a mirror. It still wasn't her old
self and never would be again, but little by little she
was becoming accustomed to her looks.

Sara easily found Royce's house that evening. It
was a sedate, white-brick home with a lovely green
lawn. Thick dark green shrubs grew in the stone urns
on either side of the front door.

Royce answered her knock, dressed neatly in a
dark blue suit, the color casting a bluish-silver tint to
his gray hair. "Come in, come in, my dear," he said
with a smile of welcome. "And may I say you're
looking gorgeous this evening?"

"Now there's no need for extravagant lies, no
matter how kindly they're intended," Sara chided
tartly. "If you intend to feed me blarney tonight
instead of solid food, I'll just turn right around and
leave."

Royce threw back his head and laughed heartily. "I meant every word of it," he insisted, "but if you're going to be difficult, I promise I won't compliment you again."

Royce made martinis while Sara glanced around his living room with approval. It was decorated in browns and muted whites and one wall was lined with over stacked bookshelves. It was definitely a room meant for comfort rather than show and Sara could visualize the doctor alone here in the evenings in his easy chair with a book.

They made small talk over the drinks and a short time later Royce glanced at his watch and said, "Our reservation is for eight so I suppose we'd better be going now if you still want that solid food you mentioned."

Sara laughed and went with him out to his car. The restaurant that Royce had chosen was in Larimer Square and had a quaint Victorian decor.

They were seated at a table for two in a quiet corner across the room from where a pianist was softly playing a romantic tune. After ordering châteaubriand and wine the two of them chatted softly about a wide range of subjects—books, sports, even opera. Although she was herself a pop singer, Sara had always appreciated opera and it was a delight to find a kindred spirit. They also laughed and joked with each other. After a while Sara was amazed to find that she was thoroughly enjoying herself.

"Tell me, Sara," Royce insisted as he replenished her wine glass during the meal, "how is it that you're up here alone staying in a cabin? I'd think such a lovely girl as you would long since have been married and had a family."

Somehow the probing question wasn't an affront coming from Royce. Sara felt comfortable with him as though he was a friend of many years' standing instead of a recent acquaintance. Although she was tempted to tell him the truth about who she really was, she resisted the urge. Even from this kind and understanding man, she did not want pity.

She shrugged her shoulders lightly before answering. "I guess I was always too busy to settle down to family life," she said. "Although," she added in a thoughtful tone, "I was seriously considering marriage before the accident. The man I might have married died in that crash."

"I'm truly sorry," Royce said quietly.

Sara gave him a quick smile. "Yes. So am I." She shook her head. "I still don't know whether or not I would have married Pete, but all the same I miss him dreadfully. He was a very good friend. At first I couldn't bear it, the knowledge that he was gone, but life has a way of going on anyway, doesn't it?"

Royce nodded and his keen hazel eyes were serious as they held her gaze. "Yes, thank God! We can't allow tragedies to wreck our lives, Sara. We just have to keep on going in spite of them. Even try to grow from them."

She looked at him curiously. "You sound as though you've had firsthand experience yourself, Royce."

He nodded once more and took a sip of wine. "Almost twenty years ago, when I was a young doctor, I was married. We had a little girl, Angie. She was three, the most beautiful child you ever saw. She had soft blonde hair like an angel's halo and beautiful dark brown eyes." He swallowed, obviously emotional at the thought of her many years later. He went on in a husky voice. "My wife had trouble sleeping and I had prescribed her some sleeping tablets. Angie was at the busybody stage and," he paused and sucked in a deep breath, "well, you can guess what happened. One day my wife forgot to put the pills away in a safe place and Angie found them and ate them. She died that night."

"How . . . how dreadful for you," Sara stammered, sick with horror.

Royce stared straight across the top of her head as he peered back into the distant past. "My wife was inconsolable. She felt so guilty, you see. A week after the funeral she drove her car off a bridge."

"I'm so terribly sorry, Royce," Sara said, feeling too inadequate to express the depths of her own pain for his loss.

Royce's gaze returned to her face, the faraway look in his eyes faded slowly and then he suddenly smiled, dispelling the gloom. "I'm the one who's sorry," he apologized. "I shouldn't have told you." He shook his head a little. "Can't imagine why I did. It's something I never talk about. Everyone around here believes I'm a confirmed bachelor."

Sara smiled quickly and reached across the table to place her hand over his. "I'll never tell," she promised.

Royce stared at her wonderingly. "Can't imagine why I told you at all. And now it's spoiled our evening together."

"No, it hasn't," Sara said firmly. "I'm glad you told me. It's made me realize my own loss and tragedy isn't the only one in the world by any means. Other people have suffered, too. Somehow it's so easy to forget that when you're hurting yourself."

They had moved on to a lighthearted discussion of winter skiing when a few minutes later, an all too familiar voice spoke from behind Sara.

"Good evening," Doug said.

Sara turned slightly to see Doug and Carla Bellamy as Royce rose to shake hands with the other man.

"Hello, Carla, J.D.," Royce greeted. "Are you leaving or just arriving?"

"Arriving," Doug replied.

While Royce and Carla exchanged a few words, Doug glanced down at Sara. He was extremely handsome this evening in his dark dinner clothes and he seemed taller tonight, more intimidating somehow and Sara felt at a disadvantage as she sat in her chair. His eyes sought and held her gaze and she felt something of a jolt. For some reason Doug was not pleased to see her. The expression in his eyes was cold and hostile, although she had no idea why. After a moment, she glanced away and offered an uncertain smile to Carla who was now watching her with a peculiar intensity.

Royce's voice was pleasant and polite, breaking the tension that had held Sara and Doug. "Would you care to join us?" he asked.

Doug glanced questioningly at Carla and Sara held her breath as she awaited the other woman's decision.

Carla shook her head and smiled charmingly at Royce. "It's very kind of you, but you're already halfway through your dinner. Another time, perhaps?"

Sara went limp with relief as Doug seconded the refusal and the two of them went away.

Royce sat down again and smiled. "Felt I had to ask them to join us," he explained to Sara in a low undertone, "but I'm glad they didn't. It would have spoiled everything."

"I know," Sara agreed, hoping Royce could not see just how glad she really was. She had been shaken by the hardness of Doug's expression and puzzled by it as well. He had been friendly enough to her the day of Billy's party. But tonight he had looked at her as though he actually disliked her and yet she could think of no logical reason for such a drastic change in his attitude. Unless, of course, she thought suddenly, he realized now who she really was.

That possibility ruined the remainder of the evening for Sara, though she tried hard to pretend that she was still having a good time, that she was still interested in the doctor's conversation. But though she smiled and responded, her heart was hammering with a nervous fear that Doug had discovered her identity.

If that were true, she thought as she drove home late that night, then she supposed she would know it soon enough. If Doug knew who she was, she was certain he would once again order her to leave, this time with a more valid reason than before. Now that his old fiancée was here, surely the last thing he could possibly want was for another woman with whom he had had a relationship, however briefly, to be on the scene as well.

Sara neither saw nor heard from Doug during the next couple of days, and slowly she relaxed. The reason for his hostility the other night still remained a mystery but she felt certain that he had not, after all, discovered her true identity. Maybe he was furious because she had told him she was not interested in a lighthearted affair. Most likely that was it, and yet even that didn't really make any sense in view of the fact that he seemed to be renewing his relationship with Carla Bellamy. Unless, of course, she decided with some bitterness, it was his pride that had been affronted.

And I don't give a bean for his pride, Sara thought indignantly. Three years ago he had ruthlessly crushed her pride and that was something she could never forgive. That night she had desperately wanted him to make love to her. True, she had been nervous about committing her body and her feelings to a man in such a total way, but she had loved him and had thought he cared for her as much as she had cared for him. She had fully expected him to kiss away her tears, to tenderly and patiently help her over her nervousness so that she could derive as much satisfaction from their coming together as he would. Little had she dreamed that he would reject her in the heartless manner he had, and now if he was upset because she was rejecting him, she told herself it was only what he deserved.

The following morning Sara wrote a short note to Agnes and then walked down the drive to the road where she placed the envelope in the mailbox. A car came down the road and slowed to a stop beside her.

"Hi, Sara," Beth Gilly called out through the open car window. "How are you this morning?"

"Fine." Sara walked over to the car. "Are you on your way to see Billy?"

Beth nodded and glanced down at her wristwatch. "Yes. I got an early start today, though. I'm almost a half hour early." She grimaced. "Which means Wayne will still have Billy tied up with a math lesson or something."

"Then why don't you come in and visit me for a few minutes?" Sara suggested. "I'll make us some coffee."

"Sounds lovely," Beth agreed. "I'll just back up and pull into your drive."

A few minutes later both girls were seated in the living room with mugs of steaming coffee in their hands. "This is a lovely cabin," Beth commented as she glanced slowly around the room, "but don't you get lonely living out here all alone?"

Sara laughed. "Everyone asks that." She shrugged. "Most of the time I like it, but just between the two of us, sometimes I do get a little lonely." She smiled now. "However, in a week or so a friend of mine is coming out to stay with me for a couple of weeks, so I'm looking forward to her visit. Where do you live, Beth? In Lucky?"

Beth shook her head and took a sip of her coffee before replying. "No, I live in Denver and I share an apartment with my cousin."

"You have quite a drive to come up here, don't you?"

"I'm used to it," Beth said. "My patients are all scattered outside of Denver proper."

"I've been toying with the idea of getting an apartment in Denver myself once my lease here is up and I'm well again. Maybe I'll get a job and stay around here forever."

"It's a nice place to live," Beth said. "I know I wouldn't want to live anyplace else. What sort of job would you be looking for, Sara?"

Sara grimaced and set her coffee mug on a lamp table. "That's what I have yet to decide," she answered.

"Are you trained for anything?"

Sara shrugged her shoulders once more. "What I'm trained for I can't do anymore since my accident. I'm thinking about taking some sort of vocational course." She laughed. "Do you think I might learn to be a good secretary?"

"Why not," Beth said, "if you think you'd like it. Or you could train to be a nurse or a physical therapist like me."

Sara grinned and shook her head. "Nothing in the medical profession, thank you. I've spent too much time in a hospital already to make me want to take up anything like that as regular work. I'll leave that in capable hands like yours and Royce Carpenter's."

Beth laughed and threw a quick glance at her watch. "Well, I'm afraid I can't help you decide what line of work you'd like to get into today because it's time for me to go. But if you're really serious about living in Denver, I'll be glad to help you any way I can, Sara, like locating an apartment. The complex where I live is really nice."

"I'll take you up on that offer when you have time to show me around," Sara said. "Thanks, Beth."

The more she thought about it after Beth left, the better Sara liked the idea of moving to Denver. She liked this part of the country and if she must find a new job and build a new life for herself, Denver seemed as good a place as any other. She would be starting out there with at least two friends—Royce and Beth. And once she was in the city, it was hardly likely that she would ever see Doug. So all that remained was a decision about what to do with herself once she was there. It shouldn't be too difficult to find something that would interest her and provide her with a future.

On Saturday Sara slept late, and by the time she awoke, the sun was high. In the kitchen she looked out the back window toward the mountaintops, which still had snow tucked here and there into crevices and ridges. It was another beautifully golden day and she pondered over what to do with her time.

As she made toast and poured cereal into a bowl, Sara turned over several possibilities in her mind. It would have been nice to visit Kate today, but since it was the weekend there was a chance Doug might be home, so she quickly abandoned that idea. She could drive into Lucky to pick up a few items like toothpaste and milk, but that notion held little appeal. It would use up little of the day and scarcely be enjoyable. Or, she mused as she sat down to eat her breakfast, she supposed she could spend the day in Denver shopping and perhaps going to a movie.

She still had not made up her mind as she washed and dried her few breakfast dishes. But before she could finish the task, a knock sounded at the front door.

She snatched up a dish towel and dried her hands quickly before leaving the kitchen. She hoped her visitor was Kate, or maybe Beth stopping in again.

It was neither. When she opened the door, she found Billy, with the aid of his crutches, and Doug standing there.

"Good morning," Doug said with an easy smile that offered no trace of the unfriendliness he had displayed the evening they had met in the restaurant. He was dressed casually today in a pair of faded jeans and a checkered shirt. It made him look younger, less forbidding somehow, than he had appeared in his dinner clothes.

"Good morning," Sara responded automatically. She was confused and uncertain about the purpose of this visit, of Doug's casual friendliness and her gaze slid away from him to Billy, to whom she directed a welcoming smile. "Won't you come in?"

Expertly manipulating his crutches, Billy crossed the threshhold and when they were all inside, he turned to Sara with a grin. "We've come to invite you to a picnic," he announced.

"Really?" Disbelievingly, Sara's eyes sought Doug's for confirmation.

Doug's lips stretched into a smile, revealing the whiteness of his teeth against his sun-darkened face and he nodded. "Kate and Vernon are gone for the day looking at some property they're thinking of buying, so Billy and I are on our own. We're about to go into Lucky to pick up a friend of Billy's to go on a picnic with us and we both decided we'd invite you as well." He paused and his dark eyes correctly read her hesitancy. "We'd be unhappy with a refusal. Unless," he added as one eyebrow lifted quizzically, "you already have other plans?"

"Well, no I don't, actually, but—" Sara began slowly.

Doug rubbed his hands together. "Then it's settled. Go get yourself a sweater or jacket in case the air is cool down by the lake."

"What about food?" Sara asked as a few practical considerations came to mind. "I can make some sandwiches and—"

"No need," Doug cut her off. "Kate packed us a huge lunch this morning before she left."

"Then I'll just get my Windbreaker," Sara said, turning toward her bedroom.

She was already wearing her jeans, a navy blue pullover top and sneakers. So in the bedroom Sara paused at the dresser only long enough to apply a bright coral lipstick and run a comb through her hair. Then she grabbed her lightweight jacket from the closet.

When she returned to the living room, Doug was lounging lazily in a deep-cushioned chair. Billy was sitting on the piano bench, his crutches propped against the wall and he was running his fingers lightly across the ivories without pressing them. Sara crossed the room to stand beside him.

Billy looked up at her eagerly. "Do you really play the piano, Sara?" he asked. "Real music, I mean?"

Sara smiled and nodded. "Sure, I do. Not so well as before my hand got hurt, though."

"Gosh!" Billy said in an awed voice as his gaze traveled to the keyboard. "It must be awfully hard to learn to play."

"Well, it takes a lot of practice to really excel at it, but it's not too difficult to learn. Lots of boys and girls your age play quite well."

He stared at her, wide-eyed as though he couldn't believe it. "Gosh," he said again. "They sure are lucky." His voice was drenched with unmistakable longing and envy as his fingers continued to gently caress the keys.

Sara studied him thoughtfully for a moment and

then she asked quietly, "Would you like to learn, Billy?"

"Would I?" His voice rose with desire, then it flattened. "But we don't have a piano and besides, there's no one to teach me."

Sara glanced at Doug and she saw that he was listening with close attention before she looked down at the boy again. "I could teach you right here, Billy, if it's all right with J.D."

"Could I?" Billy turned eagerly toward Doug and his eyes glowed with anticipation. "Could I, please, J.D.?"

Doug met Sara's gaze. "Are you sure you want to take this on?" he asked, suddenly frowning. "After all, you came here to rest and—"

"Baloney," Sara cut in rudely. "If I didn't want to give Billy lessons, I would never have suggested it. Actually, I'd love it."

"Well—" Doug still looked dubious, despite her assurances.

"Please?" Billy pleaded. There was such a naked longing in his eyes, in his voice, that Sara swallowed hard over a lump in her throat. If Doug refused—but he couldn't be so cruel. He simply couldn't.

Apparently Doug had no defense against such an intense desire to learn than she had and after a fraction of a second of further hesitation, he grinned and nodded, "Okay, pal," he agreed. "You can take lessons, provided Sara will accept the proper payment for her services."

"Oh, no you don't!" Sara said hotly, with a light of battle glittering in her eyes. "If I wanted to make money, I could open a school. I just want to teach Billy because he's my friend. And nobody," she added emphatically, "is going to make me hang a price tag on something I want to do for my own pleasure."

Doug threw back his head and his laughter was deep and strong and vibrant. "Okay, okay!" he said at last. "Climb down off your indignation. You can have it your way."

Billy gave a shout of triumph, then pressed Sara anxiously, "When can we start?"

"How about Tuesday?" she suggested. "That way I can go to town on Monday and pick up some lesson books."

"Great!" Billy exclaimed. "Wait til I tell Larry!"

Doug rose to his feet. "Speaking of Larry, don't you think we'd better be going now that that's all settled? He is waiting for us, remember?"

After collecting Billy's friend in Lucky, Doug drove the car up a winding mountain road that provided breathtaking vistas. The two boys in the backseat chattered nonstop so that there was no opportunity for either Doug or Sara to get a word in edgewise even if they had wished to. But Sara had no such desire. She was content to gaze out the window at the ever-changing, spectacular view because now a strange shyness had overtaken her. She was acutely conscious of the man who sat only inches across the seat from her. Her senses were keenly attuned to his nearness, to his powerful leg that was so close to her own, to his hands so capably controlling the steering wheel, to even the heady scent of him—a mingled scent of tobacco and after-shave lotion. Once again she was forced to remind herself to be on guard against his compelling sexual appeal.

Their destination was a lovely spot beside a clear mountain lake. As soon as they were out of the car, the boys, eager to fish, were speculating about who would make the biggest catch of the day.

"What type of fish do you get here?" Sara asked Doug as he reached into the trunk of the car, extracted a tackle box and handed it to her.

"Mainly rainbow trout," he answered. "Want to try your luck?"

Sara shook her head. "Not really. I'd just as soon be a spectator. But if you get enough for a meal, I'd be happy to cook them."

"Fair enough," Doug said with a grin. "Hear that, boys?"

"We'll get enough," Billy said confidently.

"More than enough," Larry boasted.

"Just one thing," Sara qualified. "I'll cook, but I refuse to clean them. You'll have to do that yourselves." She shuddered. "It's such a nasty job!"

"Girls!" Billy snorted derisively.

"Sissies," his friend agreed.

Sara laughed. "I'm still not cleaning any fish!"

Doug chuckled. "You'll lose face fellas, if you don't catch anything now. I have a feeling Sara might pay you back with a few barbs of her own. Come on, let's get organized. Larry, you carry the rods and I'll carry the rest of the gear."

Doug did not bother to fish himself. He saw that the two boys were set up and then he came to sit beside Sara on the ground a few yards from the bank.

Sara eyed Billy's back with unconcealed admiration. "Just look at him," she said in a low voice. "Fishing on crutches! I don't see how he manages to cast." Indeed, it looked like an awkward process as he leaned heavily on his crutch as his arm swung back and around and the fishing line whipped across the water.

Doug leaned back against the trunk of an aspen, pulled out a cigarette and lit it. "I've discovered that it's always a mistake to underestimate Billy. That boy can do most anything he sets his mind to. He's come a long way since he was first injured."

Sara nodded. "So I've heard." She hesitated, then

added softly, "I think it's tremendously wonderful and kind of you to have taken him into your home after his father died. Not too many people would bother when it's not even a relative."

Doug shrugged and gazed toward Billy. "Nothing kind about it," he said shortly. "Billy's dad was my closest friend and I'd known and cared for Billy since he was a baby. I *wanted* him and he wanted me . . . it's as simple as that. Ooops," he added in a different tone of voice as he got to his feet, "Billy's line is snagged."

Sara watched while Doug went to untangle Billy's line and she wondered at his complex personality. What she had told him was true—he *was* kind to take in a friend's child to raise, a crippled child at that, and yet there was a darker side to the man. In that bedroom three years ago he had displayed only contempt. He had merely wanted a brief, enjoyable encounter with a girl who wouldn't expect anything beyond a single night's passion. When she had turned out to be quite different, he had treated her cruelly and hatefully.

With a determined effort, Sara thrust the disquieting memory from her conscious thoughts. This was now, today. And there was no good reason to allow the past to cloud it.

A few minutes later Doug returned to drop down beside her again. "Did you enjoy yourself with Royce the other evening?" He asked in a casual voice as he plucked a blade of grass near his booted foot.

Sara stiffened, remembering the coldness in his eyes that evening, and now she glanced warily at his profile. But it told her nothing at the moment. "Yes," she answered briefly. "I did."

Doug studiously kept his gaze on the wide stretch of blue-green lake in front of them. "I would have thought our doctor was a bit too old for you."

"As a dinner companion?" she asked incredulously, deliberately pretending to misunderstand his meaning. "I found Royce to be very interesting as well as charming."

"I meant more than a dinner companion," Doug snapped with obvious irritation.

"I realize that," Sara said, giving up pretense. "But I don't think that what I do or who I see happens to be any of your business."

"You've got a string of them, haven't you?" Doug asked abruptly.

"A string of what?" She glanced at him sharply. His face, still turned toward the water, appeared rock hard, as though it had been chiseled out of the mountain range beyond the lake.

"Men," Doug said in a clipped voice. "Royce, the man in the photograph in your bedroom, even me. Yet somehow you don't look the type to keep three very different men dangling all at the same time."

"Because of my limp, you mean?" Sara demanded through her frozen lips. She was hurt by his deliberate cruelty.

"I didn't mean that at all and you know it!" Doug returned harshly. Now he turned to gaze at her fully and his eyes glittered with anger. "I just meant your personality somehow doesn't fit the kind of woman who would flit from man to man, yet you obviously do. You bowled me over that night I almost ran you down on the road, but then you backed off and now you're seeing Royce. Then there's also the man in the photo. Who is he, anyway, and why has he allowed you to stick yourself away in a mountain cabin all alone? I'd think he would be more your type than Royce. More the right age, too."

Sara was trembling with anger and for a long moment she couldn't speak. Then with a terrible bitterness that frightened her with its intensity, she said, "I'm not looking for any man in my life. Royce is simply a friend, a very kind and nice friend and I hate you for attempting to make it into something sordid. As for you . . . that night you, I—" her voice broke and she sucked in a ragged breath before continuing, "I regret what happened. It never should have occurred at all. And as for the man in the photo, he loved me and he wanted to marry me, so I don't call that sordid either!"

"Wanted?" Doug repeated the word softly, intently. "Past tense?"

Sara jumped to her feet and turned her back on him and her head was bowed as she strained to hold back the hot tears that seared her eyes. "He's dead," she said in a muffled voice.

There was a long silence and then suddenly Doug's two brown hands came around from behind her and they rested lightly on her arms. "I'm sorry," he said gently. "I'm truly sorry, Sara. I didn't realize."

"Of course not!" she exclaimed, twisting herself free of his touch. "How could you? You had no right to know about it at all, but you just couldn't resist poking and prying, could you?"

"I got one!" Larry's excited shout sliced through the air. "I got one!"

The two who stood beneath the quaking aspen turned in time to see the boy reeling in a flopping trout and the tension between them was broken.

"Nice going!" Doug yelled encouragingly as he headed toward the water at a lope. "Keep reeling, Larry! Hang on and don't let him get off your line!"

Sara followed more slowly and by the time she reached the others, the trout was on the bank and Larry was putting him on a stringer.

For the remainder of the day a silent truce existed between Doug and Sara. Both of them carefully shied away from anything remotely personal in their conversation. This was accomplished quite easily since most of the time the two boys were within hearing.

Except for that one bad scene, Sara enjoyed the day. For lunch they all hungrily devoured the fried chicken Kate had packed for them and later in the afternoon there was enough fish to bake in foil over an open campfire for dinner.

Sara felt pleasantly tired that evening as they drove home. In town they had left both boys at Larry's house where Billy had been invited to stay the night. Although she was now alone with Doug, there was a comfortable, companionable silence between them and Sara relaxed as she closed her eyes and leaned back against the seat.

When they arrived at the cabin and the car came to a stop, Doug's amused voice broke the silence at last. "Are you asleep, my little wood nymph?"

"Almost," Sara admitted. She opened her eyes and smiled up at him, saying simply, "I need some coffee. Would you like to come in and share some with me?"

Doug returned her smile. "I thought you'd never ask," he answered.

While Sara prepared the coffee, Doug got a fire going in the fireplace in the living room. When she carried their cups in on a tray, he was relaxing on the sofa and Sara sat down beside him.

For a time they talked little. Each of them was wrapped up in utter contentment as they watched the flickering fire. But at last Sara sighed and said, "It was a perfect day. Thank you for inviting me, Doug."

"Thank you for coming," he replied. His voice held an odd note and curiously, Sara glanced toward him. There was a glittering intensity in his eyes as he frankly gazed at her and it caused her heart to skip a beat.

Without a word, Doug removed her cup from her

hand, set it on the table beside his own and then he turned back to her with a certain determination. His face bent low, close to hers as his arms went around her, pressing her close to his body just before his lips parted hers.

The warmth of his mouth on hers melted Sara. For only one brief instant she attempted to resist and when that only seemed to increase the pressure of his lips and tighten his arms about her, she gave in to the swelling tide of emotion that was flooding through her and her own arms crept up to his shoulders.

"What is it about you?" Doug whispered thickly against her hair a moment later. "I thought I was a hardened case, yet you get under my skin every time I see you. All I ever want to do is hold you and make love to you." There was an aggrieved tone to his voice.

Sara gave a shaky laugh. "You make it sound like a dreadful disease," she whispered.

"I believe it is," he agreed, drawing back only slightly so that he could smile at her. "And I'm beginning to doubt if there's a cure for it." His firm lips, incredibly soft now, found her mouth again and this time it was a kiss of passionate, consuming fervency. Doug's hand slid beneath her pullover top, up her bare midriff to cup a breast, and fire streaked through Sara.

With an aching need of her own that clamored for satisfaction, Sara pressed closer to him. Her fingers discovered the buttons on his shirt and undid them and then her hand was against his skin. Sensuous waves swept over her as her palm moved slowly across the crisp hair in the center of his chest and onto the warm skin where she could feel his heart pounding.

Swiftly, Doug pulled her up into his arms, lifted her and carried her into the bedroom. The room was in darkness and the only light there was fell across the threshold from the living room.

Gently, he lowered her to the bed. The mattress sank beneath his weight as he stretched full-length beside her and turned on his side, about to draw her into his arms once more. But for Sara, reality had crashed over her with a loud roar like a violent thunderstorm during those few seconds before he joined her on the bed. History was repeating itself. Once again Doug was ready to make love to her, but when it was over, he would go his own way with no more thought of her.

"No!" She cried shrilly. Frantically, she shoved at his hands and struggled to a sitting position. "No, not this! Go away, please!"

Now Doug, too, sat up, and through the dim light she could see incredulous anger replacing the tender expression that had been on his face. Anger, but also, astonishingly, pain. But before she had time to wonder at that, he spoke.

"You can't mean this!" Doug exclaimed. "Sara, you know you want me, too! My God, I can't be mistaken!"

"Yes!" Sobs were choking her throat, making the words ragged and uneven. "Yes, you were mistaken. I was mistaken to let you . . . to allow you to think—" She broke off, gulped for air, then continued, "I don't want you, Doug Farrell! Not ever, do you hear me? Not ever!"

With the speed of lightning, Doug was off the bed and on his feet. His dark eyes glinted like burning coals. "I guess," he grated harshly, "I did make a mistake after all. I had begun to think I wanted you forever . . . as my wife!"

He turned and an instant later he was gone.

Chapter Five

Sara was scarcely aware of the heavy traffic conges-
tion that surrounded her as she drove through
Denver on her way to the airport. She drove compe-
tently, mechanically switching lanes as needed and
keeping a watchful eye on her rearview mirror. But
her mind was not on what she was doing. For the
past week and a half her thoughts had rarely been
engaged by anything except Doug and their es-
trangement.

Now, frustrated with herself for allowing him to so
completely dominate her mind, she irritably chewed
her bottom lip and chided herself for being such an
idiot. In less than an hour she would be seeing
Agnes. If she didn't get a grip on herself right away,
her friend would immediately sense that something
was wrong. The last thing Sara wanted was for
Agnes to know anything about her relationship with
Doug.

Suddenly, she laughed aloud, but the sound was
one of bitterness, totally devoid of anything remotely resembling amusement. *What relationship?* she
sneered at herself. There was none at all.

She had seen Doug only once since that evening
that had ended so disastrously and that encounter,
too, had been a disaster as far as she was concerned.
It had been on the day of Billy's first piano lesson.
Vernon had brought Billy to the cabin and Sara had

offered to drive him home afterward since Vernon had some errands to run.

She had felt safe enough in doing it. It was midafternoon and she had not expected to see Doug at home at such an hour. But unfortunately when she had pulled the car to a stop before the front steps, Doug was coming out of the house. Her heart had lurched at the unexpected sight of him and even in her dismay, her senses had automatically registered the minute details of his appearance—the neat summer-gray suit he wore, the way the sunlight cast golden highlights to his dark hair, the firm set of his lips.

"Sara just gave me my first piano lesson, J. D.," Billy had called out happily from the car window.

"That's nice," Doug had replied as he had descended the steps and come to open the car door to help the boy out. "Right now you'd better hurry inside. Mr. Elton is waiting for you."

Billy turned to smile winsomely at Sara. "Bye," he said. "See you Thursday."

"Bye yourself." Sara had to force a smile to her lips because she was uncomfortably aware of Doug's cold attitude, even though so far he had not once looked directly at her.

As soon as Billy had vanished inside the house, Doug had turned to look down at her. His face had been carefully schooled to conceal any expression, his dark eyes inscrutable, so that she could have had no way of guessing what he had been thinking.

"Thank you," he had said politely, "for the lessons you're giving to Billy. It means a good deal to him."

Sara had shrugged lightly. "Don't mention it. I'm happy to do it." Then she had given a little laugh. "I've got too much free time on my hands, you see, so I enjoy his company."

She had thought that her reference to too much

free time would have brought a quick barb from him about letting nature take its course in driving her away, but it did not. Doug's eyes had not so much as flickered with understanding or amusement. He had merely nodded politely.

"I'm glad he's no bother to you, then. Now, if you'll excuse me, I'm late for an appointment." He had then turned his back on her and had begun to walk away toward the garage.

Unable to stop herself in her deep unhappiness over the rift between them, Sara had cried out urgently. "Doug?"

He had halted, half-turned back toward her and had said frigidly, "Yes?"

"Please, don't be this way," she had pleaded. "The other night I just—"

"The other night is forgotten," Doug had said distantly. Then, before she could have said another word, he had stridden quickly to the garage.

The memory tormented her. The withdrawn look in his eyes had told her plainly that he was through with her for good, that nothing she could ever say or do in the future would change things.

A dull ache was lodged in her throat. For days now Sara had longed to cry, but her own hurt was too deep for such easy relief. Doug had said that he wanted to marry her. She had no way of knowing whether it was true or not and that was part of her problem. It was quite likely that Doug had merely said that because he had wanted to make love to her . . . that it was his way of making her feel guilty for leading him on and then rejecting him. That explanation fitted in perfectly with his past behavior.

But what if it had been true? She shook her head and sighed. If it had been true, it certainly was not now. She would have to have been dense indeed not to have gotten his message the day she had driven Billy home. Doug was finished with her. And really, she thought wearily in self-disgust, who could blame him, regardless of his intentions concerning marriage? That night when he had held her and kissed her, she had given him every indication that she wanted him, too. She had totally forgotten her resolve not to get involved with him the instant he had touched her. She had behaved with shameless abandon and any man would have been justified in his anger when she had later called a halt. She had acted like a cheap little tease and no man could appreciate such treatment. Doug, of course, could have no idea why she had done it since he did not know who she really was. He probably believed she had done it out of some perverse sense of fun when it had not been that way at all.

But there was no way she could go to him and explain, not without having to reveal the truth of her identity. And that, she could never do. Doug would never know what her rejection of him had cost her. Since that night she had trouble sleeping and eating and already it was beginning to tell on her physically. There were grayish-brown circles beneath her eyes which she tried to conceal with makeup. In the past few days she had lost five pounds, weight she could ill afford to lose since her long sojourn in the hospital.

The worst of all was the knowledge that lay like a block of cement in her heart. That she still loved Doug. The certain realization had come to her in the wee hours of the morning after he had left her that night. She had thought for over three years that she had hated him, had *wanted* to hate him. But it had merely been a feeble defense against the truth. Now her defense was utterly destroyed and with it any semblance of peace of mind that she might previously have had.

She arrived at the airport, found a parking space at last and walked briskly across the pavement toward the terminal, as though she could somehow outdistance her morose thoughts. She was glad Agnes would soon be with her. What she needed most just now was the uncomplicated companionship of a good friend, someone who could help her take her mind off herself.

The plane was on schedule and only a few moments later Sara was being warmly embraced.

"You look wonderful," she told Agnes as they headed toward the baggage claim area. And she did. Agnes Hart, dressed in a flowered black and white dress, appeared as fresh and neat as though she had just emerged from her bedroom instead of a long, tedious flight.

Agnes' eyes raked Sara's slender frame, which was clad in beige slacks and a coffee-colored blouse. "I can't say the same for you," she said in her typically acid way. "I thought you told me you had been eating like a truck driver since you'd been here, but if you are, where's it all going? You're as boney as you were when you left the hospital."

Sara grimaced. "Don't scold, please. I'm doing my best, honestly I am."

"Hmmph!" Agnes said disbelievingly. "Living alone here as you've been doing, I'll bet half the time you don't bother to cook anything for yourself. But now that I'm here, I'm giving you fair warning that I expect well-rounded meals on the table."

Sara laughed. "I lived alone before and you never worried about my eating habits. I promise I will feed you well while you're here."

"More to the point, I expect you to eat well," Agnes snapped, having the last word.

It was late afternoon by the time they reached the cabin and unloaded Agnes' suitcases. Agnes looked off toward the mountains with an appreciative eye as they walked toward the door. "You know, I don't like you being here alone, Sara, but at least I can understand why you like it here. It *is* lovely, isn't it?"

"It is," Sara agreed. "I never get tired of the scenery." Then she added in a more practical tone, "Let's put these in your room and then I'll pour some lemonade and we can sit outside and rest for awhile before dinner."

"Sounds like an excellent idea," Agnes said with approval.

A few minutes later they settled into lawn chairs behind the cabin and as Agnes leaned back and relaxed, she sighed deeply. "This is really nice. If I don't watch myself, I might get overly fond of it here and decide to abandon the rat race altogether."

"Now you know how I feel," Sara told her.

Agnes shook her head. "No, I don't," she denied quickly. "I'm a lot older than you, so it's natural at my age to want to slow down the pace a little and think about a simpler life-style but you're too young for that. Granted, you've been through a good deal and need to recover fully before going full steam again, but you should be eager to get back to work."

"I suppose I am in a way," Sara admitted. Her eyelashes lowered over her blue eyes as she gazed thoughtfully down at the frosty glass she held. "I know that physically I'm not quite ready for a heavy pace yet, but every day I'm getting stronger. The use of my hand is slowly returning and my leg has improved a lot, too. So before long I should be able to put in a full day's work again."

Agnes brightened. "Then you're coming back to take up your career?"

Sara gave her head a negative shake. "No. I've been toying with the idea of getting an apartment in Denver and staying here permanently."

"Whatever for?" Agnes exclaimed. "What would you do with yourself then?"

Sara shrugged. "Maybe take some sort of training course—maybe even go to college." She smiled. "You know, I've been thinking that maybe I'd like to become a teacher."

"Nonsense!" Agnes bristled. "Don't be foolish, Sara. You're a singer and a very talented one at that, with a career just sitting there begging to be picked up again any day you choose. It would take you four years of school before you could teach."

"I realize all that," Sara admitted, "but I just can't see myself going back to performing."

"Just because your looks have changed somewhat," Agnes snapped impatiently. "That has no bearing on your talent, Sara! Listen, honey, you're still a very popular singer. It's your voice people love, not how you look. I told you the recording company had contacted me about the possibility of offering you a new contract."

"I'm not interested, Agnes."

Agnes sighed once more. "Sara, I could spank you. There's just no sense in this. If you were quitting to get married and raise a family I could maybe understand, but not this."

The mention of marriage reminded Sara once more of Doug. The familiar pain knifed through her. Quickly, so that Agnes would not be able to read anything in her face, she jumped to her feet and murmured, "I'd better check on my roast," and hurried toward the door.

Agnes did not mention the abandoned career again that evening. Sara was under no illusions that the subject had been closed for good, but she was grateful that Agnes had not spoiled their first evening together by continuing it. Over Sara's dinner—a roast, au gratin potatoes, salad and home-baked rolls, they talked mainly about mutual friends and acquaintances.

When the dinner was over, Agnes grinned. "You

haven't lost your culinary touch, Sara. Dinner was excellent, but I must point out that the amount you consumed was hardly worthy of a truck driver."

"*Touché*. Maybe I did exaggerate a bit in my letter but there's no need for you to harp on it," Sara retorted. "At least you can see that I'm not starving."

Agnes laughed. "All right. I'll lay off. I suppose I have been coming down pretty hard on you, but it's only because I'm concerned."

Sara softened. "You don't have to tell me that," she said huskily. "You're the dearest friend I ever had."

"Well," Agnes said briskly, "let's not get overly sentimental here. It doesn't suit my image as a tough-minded agent." She stood up and picked up her plate. "You cooked and I intend to clean, so you go get comfortable in the living room. As long as I'm here we're going to strictly divide the chores right down the middle. So close your mouth and don't argue with me."

Sara had indeed opened her mouth to protest, but now she just laughed.

"All right, boss. We'll do it your way. I'll build a fire. The nights get chilly up here."

The following morning Sara was appalled to discover how late she had overslept. Agnes would think she had become terribly lazy, besides being a lousy hostess! Yawning and stretching, she forced herself out of the bed and grinned to herself as she thrust her arms into her robe. It was Agnes' fault that she had overslept, anyway. They had stayed up talking until after two.

But when she left her room and headed toward the kitchen, she saw that the door to Agnes' room was still closed. Apparently she was sleeping in this morning, too.

In the kitchen she got the coffee started, then went to the bathroom to splash water on her face and to brush her teeth before returning to her room to dress quickly in jeans and a loose-fitting cotton shirt.

By the time Agnes joined her in the kitchen a half hour later, Sara had pancakes, sausage and grape-fruit ready to serve.

"You shouldn't have let me sleep so late," Agnes said with a chagrined expression on her face.

Sara laughed. "I haven't been up long myself and I lay all the blame on your shoulders. I never stay up as late anymore as we did last night."

Agnes yawned and reached for her coffee cup. "We'll have to mend our ways the rest of the time I'm here or I'll be a worn-out wreck by the time I go back home."

After breakfast Agnes again insisted on washing up. Sara left her to it and went to make their beds. Then she remembered that she needed to pay her utility bills. So she sat down in the living room, wrote out the checks and shoved them into envelopes.

"I'm going down to the mail box," she called to Agnes. "Be back in a minute."

She didn't hurry as she walked the short distance down the drive. It was another beautiful day with summer now in full bloom. She could hear a bird chirping somewhere nearby. A couple of squirrels were chasing each other around a tree trunk, and she paused to watch them with amusement.

When she returned to the cabin, she was surprised to find Agnes talking on the phone. "All right, that will be lovely," her friend was saying. "Yes, I'm looking forward to seeing you, too. 'Bye."

Agnes cradled the receiver and Sara could not hide her curiosity as she gazed at her.

"We've been invited out to dinner tonight," Agnes announced with satisfaction. "I've accepted for both of us. I hope you don't mind."

A sinking sensation formed at the pit of Sara's stomach. "By whom?" she asked with trepidation, although instinctively, she already knew the answer.

"My friend, Doug Farrell," Agnes said, confirming Sara's worst fears. "I mentioned your name and he says you two have met."

"Oh yes," Sara said hollowly, "we've met."

Agnes did not appear to notice Sara's paleness or agitation. "Well," she said cheerfully, "what are we going to do with ourselves today? Care to go for a walk?"

Sara struggled throughout the day to behave as normally as possible, but all the while her mind churned desperately as it sought for a convincing excuse to avoid going with Agnes that evening. How *could* she possibly go, knowing how much Doug hated her? She was positive that he no more wanted her there than she wanted to go. It was only his civility that had forced him to extend the invitation to her as well as Agnes since Agnes was her house guest.

By evening, she had her excuse. Though it might sound lame, at least it was the truth. She had a headache, a dreadful pounding in the back of her head that had been brought on by the day's worry.

When she mentioned it, Agnes needed only one searching look at her wan, colorless face to be convinced.

"You poor dear," she said sympathetically. "Why didn't you say something earlier? You didn't have to entertain me all day. Go lie down and I'll bring you some aspirin before I call Doug and cancel tonight."

"No!" Sara said sharply. "Don't do that. Just because I'm not feeling well, there's no reason to spoil your evening. You go ahead and have a good time. You know how to reach Doug's house, don't you? It's just up the road. You can drive my car."

"And what about you?" Agnes said. "You need to eat something for supper. I'll stay and—"

Sara shook her head. "I'll be fine. I'll fix myself a sandwich later and then I'll go to bed early."

Agnes frowned. "I don't know," she said dubiously. "Maybe I ought to stay here with you in case you're coming down with something more than just a headache. Are you feverish?"

"No, Mother Hen, I'm not," Sara said with some asperity. "I just probably overdid things today with all the walking we did. All I need is a little rest and I'll be good as new. Now you go on with your plans for the evening and don't worry about me."

Actually, by the time Agnes departed an hour and a half later, Sara's headache was gone. She had taken the aspirins Agnes had brought her and rested on her bed while her friend bathed and dressed. But though she admitted to feeling a little better, she was careful not to let Agnes know she was feeling perfectly fit again because then she would have lost her excuse to avoid Doug's dinner.

As soon as Agnes was gone, Sara took a quick shower and slipped into her nightgown and robe. She would fix herself a bite to eat and then settle down with a book for the evening.

She opened the refrigerator and spotted the left over roast from the night before. It would make a good sandwich, she decided, but as she reached for it, she heard someone knocking on the front door.

Agnes must have forgotten something, she thought as she closed the refrigerator and went toward the living room. Or else, still in her role as Mother Hen, she had decided to come back to check on her.

But it was Doug who stood there on the porch, not

Agnes. He was wearing a dark business suit that fitted his tall frame superbly and seemed to add to his already overpowering height.

Sara was caught off guard and felt flustered at the sight of him. "Were you supposed to come here to pick up Agnes?" she asked. "She's already left to go to your house."

"I know," Doug said in a clipped voice. "She's already there."

"Then . . . why are you here?"

"I came to get you," he answered in a voice that seemed to dare her to defy the statement.

Nervously, Sara pressed her hands together and lowered her eyes. "But didn't Agnes explain that I'm not going? That I'm not feeling well?"

"She explained all right . . . about your so-called headache," he said in such a grim tone that despite herself, Sara lifted her gaze to his face once more. Doug's eyes had narrowed to slits and his mouth was set in an angry line. "You look all right to me," he told her, "so go get dressed. We're holding dinner back for you."

"No! I won't go!" Sara flared. Her anger spread through her body like hot liquid poison. "Who do you think you are anyway, to come here and start ordering me around?" She crossed her arms in a defiant gesture and glared at him. "I don't intend to go anyplace tonight."

Doug took a threatening step toward her, causing Sara to instinctively back away from the door. Once they were inside the room, Doug kicked the door shut behind him with a violent thud. "You're coming back with me tonight even if I have to carry you out of here myself wearing that. . . ." He wagged a finger toward her, indicating her robe, "so take your choice. Do you go as you are or do you change first?"

"I don't want to go!" Sara's voice rose shrilly.

"Can't you understand and accept that? And you can't really want me there either . . . not after, not after—" Her voice faltered.

"Not after what's happened between us?" He asked with swift perception.

Sara nodded wordlessly and stared at the floor during the ensuing silence.

Finally, Doug spoke again and all his anger seemed to have drained from his voice. He spoke in a low, calm manner. "Our feelings about each other are irrelevant here, Sara. Since that night you haven't come near the house and Billy's wondering why. Of course he's been coming to you for his lessons, but he's only a child and he can't understand why you've turned down his and Kate's invitations to visit them. Kate is hurt too. And now there's Agnes. We're old friends, Agnes and I, and unless you've confided in her, she's going to be doing a lot of wondering herself about why you won't have anything to do with me. Don't you think it would be better all around if we can bury this conflict between us enough so that it won't spill over and hurt others?"

Damn Doug anyway, she thought bitterly, for being right! Sara continued to stare at the floor as though it held great interest, but after a moment she reluctantly nodded her head. "I'll go," she mumbled in a defeated voice.

"Good girl!" Doug said with hearty approval. Then, unexpectedly, he reached out a hand, his fingers gently cupping her chin as he lifted her face until she was forced to meet his eyes. A smile hovered on his lips as he said softly, "It won't be so bad, I promise. I won't bite if you won't."

His little joke won a weak, answering smile from her. "I'll go change," she said abruptly, hoping to cover the breathlessness she felt at his touch and the warming light that kindled his eyes.

In the bedroom she hurriedly exchanged her nightgown and robe for pantyhose and bra and then she pulled on a soft blue dress that brought out the blue in her eyes. With quick, deft strokes, she lightly applied her makeup, ran a comb through her hair and pulled out a pair of white sandal heels from the closet.

Doug's thick brows rose in surprise when she came back to join him. "My, but you're quick," he said approvingly. "And looking very beautiful as well. You've just made a mockery of all the women who insist they need hours of preparation before an evening out."

"Well, don't tell anyone for goodness sakes," Sara insisted sharply. "I don't want my own sex to turn on me."

Doug laughed. "It'll be our secret," he promised.

An awkward strain descended upon them like a heavy fog in the intimate darkness of the car. Sara sat as close to the door as possible to insure avoiding any accidental contact between herself and Doug. Fortunately the drive was a short one and they were soon moving up the driveway in front of Doug's home.

Sara had not previously given any thought to the oddity of Doug's leaving one dinner guest alone to her own devices while he chased after another one. But when she entered the spacious living room, it was to see that Agnes had not been left to herself at all. Several others occupied the room as well. Beside Agnes on the sofa sat Royce Carpenter. Seated in nearby chairs, cocktail glasses in hands, were Carla Bellamy and another man who was a stranger to Sara. In his wheelchair, situated near Royce, was Billy.

Doug lightly touched Sara's elbow and drew her further into the room. "You've met Carla, of course," he said, smoothly playing the part of the urbane host.

Sara managed a polite smile. "Of course. How are you?"

Carla nodded shortly. "I'm fine. And you?" She obviously did not expect a reply, however, for her gaze slid away from Sara's face, going to Doug instead.

"And this is Carla's brother, Martin," Doug went on.

The other man rose to his feet to shake Sara's hand. Now that she was face to face with him, she could see a resemblance to his sister. Though his complexion was darker than hers, there was something about his eyes and mouth that was like Carla's. "I'm pleased to meet you," he said with a bold smile and an assessing glance that traveled up and down her body.

Sara resented the man's crude behavior and she quickly tugged her hand from his and turned to greet Billy, who grinned at her with a frank welcome. "Guess what, Sara?" he asked with barely supressed excitement. "Doug's ordered a piano for me! It'll be here next week."

"Hey, that's great!" Sara said with suitable enthusiasm. Fondly, she ruffled his hair. "After that, I expect to see great strides in your progress. There won't be any excuses about not having the opportunity to practice."

"For my part," Doug teased dryly, "I expect to see him on the concert platform by the time he's sixteen at the very least."

"Aw!" Billy's face reddened with self-conscious pleasure at their attentions. "I don't know about that, but it sure will be fun to try."

Now Doug turned to Sara. "Would you like a drink?" he asked politely.

"I really think we ought to go on in to dinner,"

Carla said with a slight edge to her voice. "Your housekeeper must be furious to have her dinner practically ruined by this long wait." Her accusing gaze went to Sara, forcefully reminding them all of the reason for the delay.

"Kate won't care," Billy said quickly. "She'll just be glad Sara came after all. Won't she, Doug?" He looked up at his guardian for confirmation.

"That's right, pal," Doug said easily. "I'm sure she has everything well in hand." He glanced at Sara and gave her a quizzical smile. "Well, would you like that drink? I assure you there's plenty of time."

"Oh, no thank you," she said hastily. "I only hope I'm *not* on Kate's blacklist for delaying her dinner."

"Don't be silly," Billy said stoutly. "Kate likes *you*." With all the lack of subtlety of a twelve-year-old, Billy's emphasis on the one word, coupled with a defiant glance in Carla's direction, brought a slight tension to the room.

Doug broke it quickly. "How about you going and telling Kate we're ready, Billy."

"All right." Billy turned to Sara again. "Will you come up to my room and see me after dinner?" he asked. "I'm building some model race cars. Maybe you'd like to see them?"

"Love to," Sara agreed. "It's a date."

"May I come, too?" Carla asked. "I'd enjoy seeing what you've done, Billy."

"Sure," Billy mumbled, but with far less enthusiasm than before. "I better go," he added as he turned his chair around and quickly wheeled out of the room.

The dinner was far from ruined, even with the delay. Kate had excelled in her preparations of ham, new peas with pearl onions and a lovely summer fruit salad compote boasting fresh strawberries.

The conversation was light and varied, jumping from topic to topic. Sara was pleased to note that

Agnes seemed to be thoroughly enjoying herself. But then, she thought, it was only to be expected. Agnes was the type who easily fit into any gathering and felt right at home. She, on the other hand, was different. It was harder for her to feel relaxed around people she didn't know well and the presence of Carla and her brother somehow inhibited her. She noticed that every time Doug directed a remark to her, Carla would stare at her with hostile eyes. Her brother Martin several times attempted to engage her in conversation, but though she tried to respond easily and naturally, Sara felt a strong dislike for the man. As a result, she directed most of her own comments to Royce, who was seated at her right and she was grateful for his comforting companionship.

After dinner, while the others settled in the living room with coffee and liqueurs, Sara and Carla went upstairs to Billy's bedroom, where they both duly admired the small metal cars he was assembling. When they were completed they would be able to run by remote control. Carla was profuse in her compliments, calling Billy a "very bright little boy, indeed," but when she left a few minutes later to return downstairs, Billy stared morosely at the door.

"Old black widow spider," he grumbled.

"Billy!" Sara's voice was reproving.

Billy shrugged his shoulders. "Well, she is," he said unrepentantly. "She's chasing after Doug and that's why she's trying to be nice to me. *'Little boy.'*" His voice was scornful. "Anybody in their right mind doesn't call a twelve-year-old 'little.' Why, I'll be a teenager next year!"

"I'm sure she didn't mean to insult you," Sara soothed, trying hard to hide the amusement that was bubbling inside her.

"Well, she did!" Billy insisted. "I don't like her and I wish Doug didn't. If he marries her, it'll just ruin everything." His shoulders hunched in a dejected fashion and he dropped the small car he was holding back onto the table.

"Hey," Sara said briskly, "you're just borrowing trouble, young man. Besides, even if he does marry her, what difference would it make?"

"Maybe she wouldn't want me? Not that I blame her," he added with a sense of fairness. "I don't want her."

Sara chewed her lips thoughtfully. How had Billy picked up on the truth about Carla? That supposedly was the very reason she had broken off with Doug in the first place.

"I'm sure you're just imagining things," she said now. "If Doug does marry her, I'm certain Carla will be just as fond of you as he is. In time, if you let yourself, you'll like her as well. Now I'd better get back downstairs. See you, Billy."

"See you, Sara."

When she rejoined the others and sat down, Martin came and perched himself on the arm of her chair and leaned toward her in an intimate way. "How would you like to go out tomorrow evening, sweetheart?" he asked. "Do you like to dance?"

"Thank you, no," Sara answered, leaning away as far as possible. "I have a guest staying with me for a few weeks and it wouldn't be very polite of me to go out and leave her alone."

Martin shrugged. "Maybe after she leaves, hmm?" He grinned. "I'm sure I could show you a good time."

"Er, excuse me," Sara murmured as she got to her feet, "I think I'll get myself some of that coffee."

After she poured the coffee, instead of returning to her chair where Martin remained, she squeezed herself onto the sofa beside Royce. Agnes sat on his opposite side.

Royce smiled and said in a low voice, "We'll have

to do our best to entertain your friend while she's here, Sara. Perhaps you'll allow me to take you both to dinner and a show?"

"Love it," Sara replied, smiling up at him. "I'm pleased to see the two of you hitting it off so well."

She happened to glance up and found Doug, who was standing across the room, frowning at her. Their gazes locked and held for a long moment, her's, baffled; his, disapproving. At last Doug, in response to Carla, who was speaking to him, looked away.

What now, Sara wondered unhappily. It seemed as if she couldn't please Doug no matter what. First he was angry because she hadn't come to his dinner party, now he seemed angry because she was here.

With a determined effort to thrust him out of her mind, Sara made some light comment to Royce and Agnes. For the remainder of the evening, she carefully kept her gaze averted from Doug's face.

At eleven, the party broke up. Carla and Martin were the first to leave and the rest of them prepared to go shortly afterward.

"Can I offer you ladies a ride home?" Royce asked.

"No, thank you," Agnes said. "I brought Sara's car." She picked up her handbag. "Are you ready, Sara?"

Sara opened her mouth to speak, but before she could do so, Doug said, "Why don't you go ahead, Agnes? I'll drive Sara home myself. There's something I need to discuss with her in private."

Agnes directed a curious glance toward Sara, but then she merely nodded and moved toward the door with Royce. "I'll see you at home, then. It's been lovely, Doug. My compliments to your housekeeper for the dinner."

"Of course," Doug answered as he accompanied Agnes and Royce out of the room to the entrance hall. "We'll try to do it again when—" The remain-

der of his sentence escaped Sara as they moved out
of the room and beyond her range of hearing. Left
alone, she was too restless to sit down again so she
moved across the room and stood gazing up at a
painting on the wall, but she did not really see it. She
was too busy wondering what Doug needed to speak
to her about in private.

She did not have long to wait. In only a few
minutes he was back and her heart sank at the grim
expression that made his jaw line rigid, his mouth a
straight, uncompromising gash.

"Why don't you lay off Royce?" he demanded,
getting right to the point at once. "The man's old
enough to be your father! If you must be a flirt, can't
you at least direct it to men more your own age?"

Sara gasped. "What are you talking about? Royce
and I are only friends!"

"The hell you are!" Doug exploded vehemently.
"You're young and beautiful and Royce is as vulnerable to such a combination as any other man. Even
more so, maybe. Years ago he lost his wife and child
and since then he's never loved another woman. He
has only seen women on a casual, social basis, but
ever since he's met you, there's been a change in
him. He's interested in you, all right, and I don't
want to see him hurt! I'm tough enough to take your
cold rejections after a warm come-on and so is
Martin, if his type appeals to you. But leave Royce
alone before you do some real damage!"

In an action that was as entirely reflective as it was
instinctive, Sara's arm lifted and the palm of her
hand slapped Doug's face. The stark sound of it
immobilized them both for a moment in stunned
shock. Then slowly, Doug lifted his own hand to
gingerly touch the growing red spot on his face and
his eyes glittered dangerously as he glared at her.

"I . . . I'm sorry." Sara swallowed hard and
backed a step away from him. "I . . . shouldn't have

done that," she conceded in a hesitant voice, "but you had it coming! You have no right to judge me, Doug Farrell, or to make sweeping assumptions about things that don't concern you! I know what I'm doing and Royce understands me. I have no intentions of leading him on and then rejecting him like you've done to women yourself."

"Exactly what does that mean?" Doug asked in a voice that terrified Sara in its awful, deceptive softness.

She was frightened, too, because stupidly, she had once again almost given herself away. Shakily, she turned without replying so that her back was to him, and that was her next mistake.

His fingers clamped down on her shoulders like a steel vise, hurting her so that she had to bite her lip to keep from crying out. "Don't ever turn your back to me when I'm talking to you," Doug stated in a cruel voice. "And don't you ever try hitting me again either, or you'll get more than you bargained for. And now . . . explain what you meant just then about *me* rejecting women. You rejected me the other night, remember, so on what do you base your accusation?"

Nervously, Sara struggled to free herself from the punishing pressure of his hands on her shoulders and after a moment, he released her. She sucked in a deep breath and half turned toward him, carefully keeping her eyes on his tie clasp.

She licked her lips and pressed a humorless smile to her lips. "I was just guessing, of course," she lied, hoping she sounded convincing. "But as ruthless and cruel as you can be, I'm certain it's the truth. And *now,*" she injected an impatient note into her voice, "can we please end this distasteful conversation and will you take me home?"

Chapter Six

"Get the phone, will you, Agnes?" Sara shouted from the kitchen. She was in the process of unloading bags of groceries and putting the food away while Agnes was in the bedroom hanging up clothes. They had only a few minutes earlier returned from a trip to Lucky where they had done the laundry and had gone shopping.

"Sure," Agnes called back and an instant later the ringing stopped.

Sara was trying to decide between steak and chicken for dinner that evening when Agnes came into the room.

"Royce is on the phone and wants to know if we'd like to have dinner at his house tomorrow night and then play bridge with some of his friends."

Sara, holding the packages of steaks in her hands, looked up absently. "What? The bridge is out again?"

"Really, Sara," Agnes snapped irritably, "for the past two days your mind has been a thousand miles away." With obvious exasperation, she repeated what she had previously said.

"Oh, you go ahead," Sara answered, "but count me out. I'm not good at bridge."

"But we're both invited," her friend stated. "I won't go if you don't."

"Nonsense." Sara had decided on the steaks and now she opened the refrigerator and thrust them inside. The chicken would go into the freezer. She turned to pick it up from the table and added over her shoulder to Agnes, "Of course you'll go. I'll drive into town with you, drop you off and then go to a movie or something."

"Are you sure?" Agnes asked anxiously. "That doesn't sound like much of a fun evening for you. Maybe I should refuse and—"

Sara placed her hands on her hips and glared. "Agnes Hart, you love to play bridge and you know you'd enjoy the evening, now wouldn't you?"

"Well, yes, but—"

"No buts," Sara laughed. "Just go tell the man you'll be there, will you?"

At last Agnes went and Sara continued to put away her groceries. Agnes had been right about her absent-mindedness the past couple of days ever since Doug had pitched into her about Royce and she had slapped him. Would she never get the ugliness of that scene out of her mind?

It made no sense, she told herself scornfully, that she could love such a man, and yet she did. It had hurt unbearably for him to call her a cheap little come-on and to assume she was out to hurt every man by that sordid little game. Doug's opinion of her was lower than the ground, proving beyond all doubt that whatever he had felt for her, it had definitely not been love. Not as she defined the term, anyway. Doug had behaved horribly toward her without any logical reason.

Not that she had behaved any better, she thought with shame, lashing out as she had done and slapping him. If name calling and physical violence was what love reduced people to, then she was better off without it. It was just unfortunate that Agnes should be friends with Doug and want to socialize with him.

Perhaps for the remainder of the visit, she could manage to keep herself out of any further contact with Doug.

During the day she had the happy thought that maybe she could meet with Beth in town tomorrow night while Agnes was at Royce's. In the evening she telephoned to see if it would be convenient and Beth sounded pleased. "I'd love it, Sara. My cousin will be out for the evening and I'll be all alone, so I'll enjoy having a visitor."

The sun was still high in a cloudless sky the next evening when Sara parked her car in Royce's drive.

"Won't you come in with me just long enough to say hello?" Agnes asked with an oddly nervous note to her voice.

Could her old friend be suffering from a sudden attack of shyness? Sara wondered incredulously. Agnes looked quite lovely this evening in a lavender dress with a matching jacket, which was accented by only a single strand of pearls. But despite her self-contained neat look, her hands betrayed her by twitching in her lap.

"Sure," Sara agreed easily, "I guess I've got a few minutes to spare."

Royce's welcome was cordial, but understated a bit, as though perhaps he, too, was a little ill-at-ease about the intimate dinner he was about to share with a lady he hardly knew.

"How about a drink, Sara?" he offered. "And won't you change your mind and stay to dinner with us?"

Sara shook her head. "No thank you to both questions, Royce. Beth is expecting me, so I can only visit a moment."

But the few minutes were well spent, she decided when she returned to the car with a tiny smile hovering on her lips. She had chatted idly about

Billy, the unusually hot weather and the latest doings in Congress and before she left Royce and Agnes were cheerfully arguing politics. Maybe, Sara thought as she drove away, romance was tough at any age.

Beth met Sara at the door of her apartment wearing faded jeans and a floppy shirt, a far cry from the customary neat uniform she wore on her job.

"Hi," she greeted breezily. "Hope you like pizza. I ordered a couple of them for us and bought a bottle of wine."

"Sounds great," Sara replied. "I like your place," she added as she glanced around the room which was gaily decorated with numerous wicker baskets and potted plants.

"Thanks," Beth grinned. "I'm a plant freak in case you haven't noticed." She waved a hand toward the sofa. "Have a seat, Sara, and I'll pour us each a glass of wine."

In a short time, Beth returned with their wine and she sank down in a chair opposite Sara. For a while they talked easily of Beth's job and Sara's idea of perhaps studying to be a teacher.

The pizzas arrived and Sara, who had eaten a sandwich at home earlier, was surprised to find herself hungry.

"I'm sorry Kim isn't here to meet you," Beth said a little later as they cleared away the remnants of their meal. "She's out with her fiancé."

"Oh? When's the wedding?"

"Not until after Christmas," Beth answered as she carried their plates into the kitchen. "Hugh wants to save up a little money before they get married."

"He sounds like a sensible person," Sara said thoughtfully. "Do you like him?"

Beth nodded. "He's a nice guy." Then she grimaced. "But he *is* going to be stealing away my roommate." She suddenly directed a level gaze at

Sara. "Maybe when the time comes, if you're still interested in living in Denver, you might consider moving in here with me and sharing expenses?"

"I just might at that," Sara said as they returned to the living room with fresh glasses of wine. The idea appealed to her. "That's about when my lease will be up on the cabin. But, Beth, let's be honest," she insisted. "Are you sure that by December you'll still be single yourself?"

Beth flushed and stared down into the deep ruby-red liquid in her glass. "You mean Wayne?"

Sara nodded. "I'm not trying to be nosy or anything," she said quickly, "but you two *do* have something going, don't you? Maybe by that time you will—"

Beth shook her head and dropped down onto the opposite end of the sofa. "*Did* have something going," she said in a low voice. "Wayne broke off with me last night, Sara."

Sara was appalled. "I'm sorry, Beth. I would never have said anything if I'd had any idea!"

Beth waved a hand as though easing Sara's embarrassment. "No, it's okay, really. In fact, if you don't mind, maybe it'll do me some good to talk about it with someone. I haven't been able to bring myself to tell my folks or Kim yet."

"Then talk away," Sara said quietly.

Beth stared off across the room toward the window. "Wayne's parents own a farm in Georgia and his father is sick. They've got a lot of debts, too." She shrugged her shoulders. "Anyway, Wayne has decided he has to go home and take over things there. In three weeks he'll be done with Billy's summer schedule and, as you know, when school starts in the fall, Billy will be going to public school. So Wayne's not going to sign a new teaching contract with the district this year. In less than a month, he'll be going back to Georgia for good."

"I see," Sara said slowly. "I'm sorry. But . . . I don't understand, Beth. If Wayne loves you, why hasn't he asked you to go back with him?"

"Wayne is proud," Beth said bitterly. "I know he cares about me, though he's never actually said he loved me in so many words and he's never actually proposed either. Somehow I just took it for granted that sometime, sometime . . . well, anyway," she added after taking in a shuddering breath, "he says that it wouldn't be fair to me to keep up a relationship any longer, that he's going home to a lot of problems and that he's in no position to be able to afford a wife and might not be for years. So . . . it's just over between us."

"What did you say to all that?"

"What could I say?" Beth asked as she wiped a wayward tear from her cheeks. "Wayne doesn't care enough about me to want me at his side 'for better or for worse.' If he did, he wouldn't be leaving like this! I'm strong and healthy. I can work too, can't I? Isn't that what marriage is all about . . . working through problems together? But he didn't ask . . . he just told me how it's going to be!"

"I'm sorry," Sara murmured again, knowing the words were totally inadequate, yet not knowing what else she could say.

"Yes." Beth managed a wan smile. "So am I . . . sorry I ever even met him! Love isn't worth all the hassle!"

"I'll toast to that!" Sara laughed shortly and held out her wineglass in the traditional gesture.

Beth leaned forward, clicked her glass against the edge of Sara's, took a sip and then asked curiously, "Some guy hurt you, too?"

"Of course," Sara replied in a dry voice. "Doesn't it happen to every girl sooner or later?" She gave her slender shoulders a careless shrug. "Only mine didn't even have a good-sounding excuse like Wayne's. All he wanted was an affair, nothing permanent. When I got serious, he got scared . . . and angry."

"The rotten bum!" Beth declared morosely.

"Yes." Sara nodded her agreement, then thought of the man who would raise a friend's child, a man who, though he wanted her out of his cabin, would bring her firewood, a man who checked up on her in a storm and she added softly, "Though he does have his good points, too."

"You still love him, then?' Beth asked.

"Yes, darn it, I do." She set her glass down on a table and smiled. "Let's change the subject to something more pleasant," she suggested.

"Let's do," Beth agreed quickly. "No point in ruining our entire evening."

It was past ten before Sara set out on the long drive back home. Royce had told her he would drive Agnes back himself and as she drove through the night, Sara was glad to be alone. After the shared confidences with Beth, she was in a thoughtful mood and was glad she did not need to make conversation with anyone, even Agnes. Right now she felt sorry for Beth, sorry for Wayne and sorry for herself as well. Why did life—and love—have to be so complicated?

The first week of Agnes' visit slipped by quickly and pushed into the second. After that first evening of bridge with Royce, Agnes saw him several more times. One evening he came to dine with the two of them at the cabin and another, Agnes made the long drive to Denver and back in order to attend a concert with him.

The day following the concert, after which Sara had heard Agnes drive home quite late, Sara teased,

"You know, Agnes, I do believe there's a new glow about you. Is it the mountain air or Royce's attentions?"

They were sitting outdoors where Agnes had been in the process of writing a letter while Sara studied a cookbook for a good cake recipe.

Now Agnes closed her stationery notebook with a little snap. "The air, no doubt," she said as her irascible temper flared and heightened her color.

"No doubt," Sara agreed solemnly, but there was a devilish twinkle in her eyes as she added, "although I've heard that love can affect people that way, too."

"Don't be outrageous!" Agnes ordered sternly. "The man is simply a very nice companion as you well know. Besides, we invited you to come along with us last night, too. Does that sound like romance to you when two people don't mind a third party coming along?" Impatiently, she got to her feet and without giving Sara time to reply, stated with dignity, "I'm going inside to call the office. No telling what's been going on there in my absence."

Sara stayed where she was, enjoying the slight breeze that caressed her skin. She really shouldn't have teased Agnes about Royce, she supposed, feeling a slight twinge of guilt. But it had been irresistible. Ever since Walter's death Agnes had concentrated exclusively on her work in her own particular way of dealing with her grief and men had been far down on her list of priorities. It was good for her, meeting Royce like this, Sara decided. The block of ice that had frozen around Agnes' heart at the loss of her husband was gradually thawing. She was a wonderful person and it would be a shame if she lived out the remainder of her life alone when she had so much love to offer a man.

Not, Sara mused, that she expected things to come to such a pass between the doctor and her friend.

After all, in another week or so Agnes would be going back to L.A. and her busy life there while Royce would be here. But at least meeting someone warm and genuine like Royce would wake Agnes up to the fact that there were some nice men left in the world. It might encourage her to accept other men's social invitations and, in time, maybe she would meet someone worthy of taking the place of her beloved Walter.

Realizing the futility of her speculations concerning Agnes' love life, and the sheer irony of it since she was totally unable to handle her own, Sara grimaced to herself, got up and headed toward the cabin. It was almost lunch time and she ought to do something about preparing it. In a couple of hours Billy would be arriving for his piano lesson.

"How are things at the office?" she asked a half hour later as she sat across the table from Agnes.

Agnes poured dressing over her green salad. "Pretty well, it seems. By the way," she said very casually, "Rudy says the recording company has been in touch again about you. He also thinks we could line up a TV special for the Christmas season."

Sara unconsciously tugged at a strand of her hair. "Please," she begged unhappily, "let's don't go over all that again. We've been having a lovely time together, so let's not spoil it now."

Agnes pressed her lips into a reproachful line and her brow furrowed. "Billy's coming for his lesson again today, isn't he?"

Sara nodded.

"Is that enough for you?" Agnes demanded. "Living out here alone and the highlight of your week is giving piano lessons to one child?" She shook her head. "I'm not saying Billy isn't a great boy, Sara, he is, and I'm glad you're helping him. But there's more to life than this!" Her hand waved

in an arc, indicating the room. "Your leg is better
. . . you only limp now when you're extremely tired.
I've noticed that your hand is almost back to normal
and even your hair is beginning to grow out. There's
no reason for you not to come back and take up your
career."

Sara lowered her lashes so that they shielded her
eyes. "I'm sorry . . . but I can't. Not yet, anyway."

"All right," Agnes said with a sigh, "stay here
another month or so, get totally fit again, but," she
stipulated, "promise me that before you embark on
a hair-brained scheme like getting a job or studying
to be a teacher, you'll at least seriously consider
coming back to your singing again. Honey," she
added with desperate appeal, "it's the only thing
you're qualified to do and it's just plain silly to give it
up."

Sara laughed suddenly. "You make it sound like
some dull, dead-end job and that the only thing it
has to recommend it is security."

Agnes grinned. "Maybe I did at that, but the truth
is you've got a talent that you've got no *right* to
throw away."

Royce invited them both to dine with him at the
Country Club on Agnes' last night there a week later
and this time, Sara did not refuse to accompany
them as she had on all the previous occasions. For
one thing, both Royce and Agnes insisted she come
along and, for another, she was heartily tired of
sitting alone most evenings.

Sara and Agnes both bought new dresses for the
evening and for the first time in months, Sara was
truly satisfied with her appearance. The floor-length
dress was sheer layers of muted swirls of black and
white, lending her an almost exotic appearance.
Agnes was equally elegant in a long oyster-white
dress with a pearled bodice.

When the knock sounded on the front door and Agnes gracefully crossed the room to answer it, Sara said in a stage whisper, "You're so gorgeous tonight, Royce will probably propose."

Agnes made an inelegant face at her and whispered back, "Shut up and behave yourself," before, with a prim expression now on her face, she opened the door.

Royce entered the room and following closely behind him was Doug, immaculate in a dark suit and pale blue tie. Sara's eyes widened with confused surprise at the sight of him and as though drawn by a magnet, his gaze swiftly met hers.

While Royce was greeting Agnes, Doug's long stride carried him straight to Sara. "Good evening," he said in a soft voice.

"Good evening," she responded automatically.

"Surprised to see me?"

"Very," she admitted. "Why are you . . . ?" she began.

Doug smiled winsomely and it was as though a breath of fresh air swept through the room. "Royce told me he didn't think his heart was up to the strain of dining out with two beautiful women alone this evening, so he invited me to come as well. Do you mind?"

"Mind?" Sara repeated, parrot-fashion. "No, of . . . of course not."

There was some quality about him tonight, something intense in his eyes that made her feel wary as well as a bit breathless, as she lowered her gaze to her clasped hands.

"You're looking extremely lovely this evening," Doug said in almost a whisper. "I wish I could believe it was all for my benefit, but there's no chance of that, of course." The timbre of his voice was deep and it seemed to hold a hint of some pain Sara could not understand.

"How could it be," she countered, lifting her gaze to his, "when I didn't even know you would be here?"

"Meaning," he asked swiftly, "that it would have been for my benefit had you known?" His dark eyes once again held hers with a strange, fierce power.

Sara gave her head a tiny shake. "I don't know," she admitted in a whisper. "After . . . after that night, I thought—" Her voice trailed away miserably at the memory.

Doug's hand came out to cover both of hers with a gentle touch. "Forget that night," he said urgently, still in that low, compelling voice that could not reach Agnes and Royce across the room. "Let's enjoy this evening together, shall we?"

For a long moment Sara's wide blue eyes searched his face for some hidden intent. But there could be no doubt of the sincerity in his voice, the genuineness of his words and finally she nodded and smiled. "All right," she said softly. "I'd like that."

Doug's hand tightened over hers. "That's my girl," he whispered approvingly.

Dinner at the club was lovely and the four of them enjoyed it thoroughly. Sara was aware that the wine with dinner was partly the reason she felt so relaxed and happy, but deep inside she knew that the major reason the evening seemed so perfect, the food so delectable, the table conversation so scintillating was the fact that Doug was there. Every time she happened to look up, he would be watching her with a smile on his lips and a warmth in his eyes that melted her bones. Her logical mind told her that there was danger in allowing her happiness to be so dependent upon his presence, upon his obvious admiration. But she didn't care. She loved him and tonight she was happy and for the moment that was enough. Tomorrow could take care of itself.

After dinner, while they had coffee, the lights

dimmed. From across the vast room, a combo began playing a soft, romantic tune.

Almost immediately, Doug leaned over and asked, "May I have this dance?"

Mutely, Sara nodded and a minute later they were on the dance floor. Doug drew her into his arms and she could feel the heat of his hand on her back through the thin fabric of her dress. Then he lowered his head until his face was touching hers and he pressed her closer, molding her pliant body to his hard frame.

Sara's heart tripped as tumultuous emotions swept through her. Her entire being was attuned to his nearness; to the masculine scent of his after-shave lotion, to the fine texture of his face against the softness of hers, to the perfect rhythm of their swaying movements.

When the music came to an end, Doug released her and Sara had a sense of being bereft. But Doug, taking her arm, led her not back to the table as she had expected, but through a wide door that opened upon a terrace.

There was no one outside except themselves and still without speaking, Doug led her down the steps into the formally laid out garden.

The garden path wound its way between hedges and flower beds. The darkness shielded all but their shadowy shapes and the faint scent of some flowering plant's sweet perfume.

Once they were totally out of sight of the lighted club building, Doug stopped and gently gathered Sara into his arms.

His kiss, when it came, was tender and warm, rendering her helpless to resist, even if she had wanted. Desire welled up from the depths of her soul and her lips parted in absolute surrender.

"Sara," he murmured huskily as his mouth traveled to the delicate lines of her throat, "my sweet little wood nymph." He lifted his head and their faces were very close. In the darkness she could only see the glow in his eyes before he bent his head to once again claim her soft lips.

This time the kiss was demanding, almost devouring as his starved passions sought for fulfillment. His hand caressed her throat and then slipped inside her dress to touch the soft creamy skin of her breast.

His action inflamed Sara's senses, like an uncontrollable forest fire. She caught her breath sharply. Her nerve ends tingled in an agony of unsatisfied desires as his hand gently stroked her breast. Her own fingers slid through his thick hair and then down to his neck and her touch seemed to ignite his passions even more, for he crushed her tightly against his chest.

"We've got to get things settled between us, one way or another," he whispered shakily a moment later as his hand gently tucked her hair behind her ear. "We can't go on like this, Sara, hot one time, cold another. It's driving me insane!"

"I know," she answered in a choked voice. "Me, too."

"Then let's find a bench somewhere and sit down and discuss this," he suggested softly. "Unless it's too chilly out here for you?"

"No, no, I'm fine," she assured him. And she was, as long as his arms were about her. The warmth of his body radiated heat over and through her so that she was oblivious to the sharp night air. "I . . . I want to talk this out, too." She had suddenly come to the conclusion that the time had come to quit playing games, to tell him who she really was before things went a single step further between them. Tonight, for the first time, she felt she could.

Unfortunately, with dreadful timing, just at that moment a group of people emerged from the club, laughing and chattering. Their voices grew closer as they obviously started down the path toward the two who stood in the dark shadows.

"Damn!" Doug muttered beneath his breath.

The group rounded the bend and were suddenly upon them.

"Doug . . . here you are!" A high, feminine voice exclaimed. "Royce told us you were here so we came to find you. I want you to come inside and dance with me, darling."

It was Carla Bellamy and her brother, Martin, and another couple who were strangers to Sara.

Doug responded with a polite smile to the greetings of the others and Sara somehow managed to force her lips into some semblance of a smile as well, while in fact she felt dangerously close to tears.

"While Doug dances with Carla, may I claim the same honor with you?" Martin asked Sara. Without waiting for an answer, his hand gripped her elbow, and he was urging her back up the path.

Sara felt helpless to resist in front of the others, but she glanced back toward Doug in an effort to see what he wanted her to do.

But Doug wasn't even looking at her. Carla had both her arms snugly wrapped around one of his and Doug was smiling down at her as she spoke to him, just as though she were the most important woman in the world.

Swallowing over the tears that were thick in her throat, Sara lifted her chin proudly, stared straight ahead and allowed Martin to guide her toward the terrace and back inside the club.

Chapter Seven

The cabin was unbelievably silent and lonely the night after Agnes left. Sara had gotten quite used to her friend being out almost every night with Royce, but this was different. Tonight she would not be coming in late to share a cup of hot tea and recount the evening with her.

Sara didn't bother with a fire tonight. Its cheery, flickering light would only emphasize the fact that there was no one there to enjoy it with her. Besides, it would also remind her of Doug, of the night he had been here and had built one for her. They had gazed at it together over steaming mugs of coffee and the shared intimacy of conversation.

Instead, she went to bed early, propped herself up against a pile of pillows and tried to get interested in a novel. But it could not command her attention as it should have, even though it was on the best seller list. Her thoughts kept wandering to Doug and the events of the previous night.

It had ended horribly. Unhappily, Sara dropped the unread book on the bedcovers beside her. Her eyes clouded as she pictured the evening once again in vivid, painful detail.

After Carla had arrived, the magic spell that had woven around Doug and herself had dissipated. From that point on, Carla had monopolized Doug, dancing with him and sitting close beside him at the table at other times. As far as Sara could determine, Doug had not minded in the least. In the same way, Martin had monopolized her and Sara had allowed it only because she had been so miserable. The other couple, a young married pair who were friends of Carla's, had seemed happy enough talking with Royce and Agnes, and Sara was grateful that Agnes' attention had been so engrossed by them because she did not seem to notice the change that had come over her or Doug.

Once, toward the end of the evening when Carla had gone off to the powder room, Doug had asked Sara to dance again. But by that time she had been not only hurt, but angry as well, and had felt that Doug was trying to throw her a crumb of his company while he happened to have a free moment. She had curtly refused and with cold deliberation, had turned to Martin beside her, given him her brightest smile and had asked him some question which she could no longer recall now. But the action had served its purpose. Doug had not approached her again and by the time the party had broken up at last and the two of them were in the backseat of Royce's car together, neither had attempted to speak to the other. Doug had sat as far on his side of the seat from her as possible, while she had hugged her own side in the same way.

Maybe Agnes was right, she thought as she folded her arms behind her head and stared at the bedroom ceiling. Maybe she should just pack her bags and head back to California. It would get her out of Doug's vicinity. Then perhaps she could get on with the business of living again and get away from the tangled emotions that the very sight of him brought forth. Perhaps she should go back and attempt to pick up the shreds of her career once more. At least it would keep her so busy she would rarely have time to dwell on her personal disappointments.

Abruptly, she reached out and switched off the lamp, plunging the room into darkness. She would sleep on the idea, she told herself wearily. But one thing was certain—Denver or Los Angeles, she was going to have to make up her mind soon because she could not go on living here in Doug's cabin any longer than necessary. She never wanted to see him again and that would be impossible as long as she remained his tenant. Since he had been trying to get rid of her ever since she had arrived, she reminded herself bitterly, it should be easy enough to get back the remainder of the money from the unused portion of her lease.

By morning, Sara felt an inner calm that she had not experienced for a long time. Before breakfast, after dressing in slacks and a lightweight pale blue sweater, she made her way down the hill to the creek. The cold, tumbling water chilled the air far more than it had a few weeks ago and she couldn't help but think that fall would soon be here, and then the winter snows would come and she would not be here to see it as she had planned. It was a disappointment, but one she would have to accept, because when she had awakened this morning, she had known her answer at last. She would be going back to California.

As usual, Agnes had been right. It would be foolish for her to remain in Denver, to go to school four long years in order to become a teacher. What if she wasn't suited for it? But she did have a talent for singing and if Agnes' prediction was on target, the public would still accept her because of her voice and not for the looks she used to have. It was high time she got over her extreme sensitivity about her changed appearance, accept herself for what she now was and expect others to do the same.

When she returned to the cabin, before she could lose her nerve, she picked up the phone and dialed

Doug's house. The moment she told him she was leaving the die would be cast and there could be no wavering, no backing out.

Kate answered and when Sara asked for Doug, she said, "J.D.'s not here. He left yesterday afternoon on a business trip and he'll be gone for a week."

"I see." Disappointment washed over her. Now the inevitable would just have to be postponed. But Kate was still on the line and she had to add something. "It wasn't important, anyway. I'll just talk to him when he returns."

"Sure," Kate agreed with a lack of curiosity. "Say, if you're not busy today, why don't you drop by for awhile? We haven't seen you lately."

"I'd love to," Sara said promptly.

Beth had already come and gone when Sara arrived that afternoon. But Wayne was there and after he finished his lessons with Billy, he joined the two women for coffee in Kate's kitchen.

"Wayne's leaving us in another week or so," Kate told Sara. "He's going back home to Georgia."

"Is that right?" Sara asked, pretending complete ignorance.

Wayne nodded and absently stirred his coffee. "My folks need me to run the farm. Dad's not doing very well right now."

"I'm sorry to hear that," Sara replied, "but I hope things work out for you."

"Yes," Wayne said glumly, "so do I. This isn't something I want to do. I just feel I have to do it."

The topic of conversation changed after that, but Sara noticed that Wayne remained morose, entirely unlike his usual light-hearted self. She couldn't help but wonder if it was entirely due to his concern about his parents and the unwelcome change he was making in his own life or if it also had something to do with Beth.

As soon as he finished his coffee, Wayne did not linger but bid them both goodbye and left.

Kate refilled Sara's and her own coffee cups and sighed. "That boy is about as happy as a man who's just been told he has three months to live."

"I noticed," Sara admitted.

"The thing is that Wayne feels pulled in two directions," Kate explained. "He feels it's his duty to go home and take over his father's affairs, but on the other hand he wants the freedom to get on with his own life as well. I think he must have had a falling out with Beth, too. I've noticed lately that they have very little to say to one another."

Sara said nothing. Apparently Beth had not confided in Kate and she knew she had no right to mention what she had been told. She picked up her cup, took a sip, and asked instead, "What have you been up to lately? I think Doug told me that you and Vernon have been looking at some property?"

Kate's face brightened. "Didn't I tell you? We bought a hundred acres of land. The paperwork's being processed now."

"How wonderful for you! Where is it located?"

"About forty miles south of Denver. We're so excited about it, Sara. A place of our very own at last. Vernon's gone right now pricing trailer houses. We figure that's what we'll live in at first until we get our cattle and start making the place pay for itself. Later on we'll build a house."

"When do you think you'll be moving, then? And what about Billy?"

Kate's face sobered. "J.D. will have to hire someone else to stay here and not just everyone wants to live this far away from the city. But he'll have plenty of time to find someone he likes. Vernon says we probably won't be set up to actually live on our place before the first of the year."

"What does Billy say about it?" Sara asked curiously.

Kate smiled. "Ah, Billy's such a good kid. He says he doesn't mind about our leaving if we do two things: one, get someone here he can at least tolerate," she laughed, adding, "his words, not mine, and second, if he can come and visit us sometimes during his school vacations. He's already figuring out ways he'll be able to help Vernon with the work. And you know, he'll do it, too. I never met a less handicapped boy in my life. Know what he did yesterday? That dog of his ran off and got his leg tangled up in some brush and rocks about a half a mile from here. Without telling us, Billy went off alone on his crutches to find him and when he did, he somehow managed to move a large rock to free the little rascal. When he got home, his shirt was torn and he had a couple of bruises, but he sure was proud of himself, and frankly, so were we!"

Sara laughed. "He's got spunk, that's for sure. You know, I think Billy is—"

Her words were cut off as the telephone rang.

Kate got up and crossed the room to the wall telephone, commenting over her shoulder, "That's probably Vernon saying he'll be late for dinner."

Kate was smiling as she spoke into the telephone, seemed surprised and delighted to hear from whomever was on the other end of the wire, but a moment later the smile was wiped away and her face went white.

"Oh, no! What happened?" she exclaimed. Then after listening for a moment, asked, "Do the others know?" and after another silence, added, "No, Vern isn't here just now, but he should be home soon. I'll have him call you the minute he gets in, but in the meantime I'll check the airlines and see how soon we can get seats. Yes, all right, bye."

Sara had risen to her feet and as soon as Kate hung up the receiver, she went to her and took her limp hands into hers. "Are you all right, Kate?" she asked quietly. "What is it?"

Kate's face crumpled, then. "It's Vern's mother," she said, close to tears. "She died of a heart attack about an hour ago." She jerked one of her hands free from Sara's and ran it agitatedly through her hair. "Oh, why isn't Vern here now? What am I going to say to him, Sara?" Distractedly, she glanced toward the counter. "Where's the telephone directory? I must call the airport."

"You've had a shock, Kate," Sara said gently. "Come sit down and I'll call the airport for you. Where must you go?"

"Birmingham." Kate allowed herself to be thrust back into her chair. "Vern's brother will meet us there and drive us the rest of the way. I'll need to pack and—"

"Don't worry," Sara told her. "I'll help you. Let me get your reservations first." She located the directory in a drawer, laid it on the counter and began flipping through the pages.

"And what about Billy?" Kate asked suddenly. "J.D. is gone." She turned to gaze pleadingly at Sara. "Will you come and stay here with him? I don't know just how long we'll be away, but if we're not back by the time J.D. is, maybe he can find someone to stay temporarily."

"Of course I'll stay with Billy, Kate," Sara promised. "Don't worry about a thing." She had no time at all to consider the wisdom of the promise or to wonder how Doug would react to the discovery of her being installed in his house when he returned. She only knew it was something she had to do.

Three hours later Sara and Billy waved goodbye to Kate and Vernon. Vernon had returned shortly after Sara had booked their flight for early evening and despite his shock and grief, he had efficiently attended to some necessary chores before they left while Kate and Sara packed. He and Billy fed the horses and the dog, checked all the locks on the windows and doors and then Vernon instructed Sara about such matters as where the electrical switch box was located.

As soon as they were gone, Sara and Billy drove to her cabin where she made short work of packing a few clothes and locking up.

They cooked hot dogs for dinner, Billy's choice, naturally, and later in the coziness of Doug's study, they played twenty questions until finally Billy exclaimed in disgust, "I gave you plenty of excellent clues, Sara, and you *still* didn't guess mastodon."

Sara sneered indignantly. "Excellent clues, indeed! Who in the world knows what a shovel-tusker is, anyway?"

Billy's eyes held a devilish, triumphant gleam. "Mr. Elton does," he told her. "How do you think I found out?"

"Well, I never had a Mr. Elton in my life and what you are," Sara scowled at him, "is an obnoxious young genius who likes to show off! And since you can't play fair, I suggest we both go to bed."

Billy laughed. "Might as well if you're gonna be crabby about it," he agreed, not in the least put out by her insults. "Even sleep is better than such a dull game. By the way, Sara, I've got this great book about prehistoric animals if you'd like to bone up." Sara shook a menacing fist at him and chuckling, he turned his wheelchair in the direction of the elevator that had been installed near the stairs just for his benefit. "Okay, okay," he added quickly, "I'm going. Goodnight, Sara."

Sara smiled. "Night, Billy. If you need me, I'll be sleeping in the bedroom across the hall from yours."

It was still far too early to think of sleep, Sara

decided after a quick glance at her watch. It was only a little after nine. She knew if she went to bed now she would only toss and turn for hours. Billy had his own television set in his room and she imagined that he would entertain himself by watching it for awhile before he fell asleep. But though there was a television set here in Doug's study, too, she felt too restless to watch a program.

Instead, she gazed around the room with interest. Tonight was the first time she had ever been inside this room and she had to admit to herself that it was a wonderfully comfortable and peaceful room. The knotty pine paneling and polished woodwork gleamed in the lamplight. There were bookcases lining two walls and a desk was centered at the opposite end of the room. In between was a brown and gold tweed sofa and set at right angles to it, two tan leather chairs. Against the wall opposite the door was a rock fireplace and Sara could imagine Doug alone here in the evenings, a fire crackling in the hearth as he relaxed and enjoyed his solitude. The room showed a sensitive side of him that she had only rarely been privileged to glimpse.

Idly, she went over to the bookcases to view the titles. As she expected, there was a large selection concerning electronics. There were also volumes on ranching and agriculture, books on world history and a number of biographies. But as far as Sara could determine, there was little or no fiction. She supposed wryly that Doug was too matter-of-fact for that.

Moving on, she saw his stereo and tape deck unit on a wide lower shelf and this caught her interest. There was a cabinet below in which she supposed he kept his records and tapes, and after only a moment's hesitation she opened the doors. Surely Doug would not object to someone listening to his music.

She dropped to her knees on the carpeted floor

and began sorting through the large collection of albums. Doug's taste, she soon discovered, was eclectric. There were selections of symphonic music and jazz, pop and western.

And then shock electrified her as she opened a second cabinet. There, to her disbelieving gaze, was a complete collection of every recording she had ever made! Her hands trembled as she pulled them out to look at them. *Sheila Starr in Concert; Sheila Starr's Moonlight Magic; Sheila Starr's Favorites.* There were a number of singles as well of her top hits.

Was it just coincidence that he had them? she wondered. Was it just that as a music lover he had bought them to round out his collection or was there some more personal reason that Doug had bought every one of her records? Sara shook her head in bewilderment as she stared down at one of the albums. On its cover was a glamorous, totally unreal photograph of herself in a flaring white gown, a deliberately hazy picture in which both her hair and skirt had a fly-away look as though she were standing in a stiff breeze.

Carefully, she stowed them back inside the cabinet the way she had found them, closed the door and got stiffly to her feet. If only, she thought dazedly, she knew what all this meant. When he had rejected her three years ago he had seemed to hate her, yet if he had, why then, had he gone to the trouble of collecting all her later recordings? It didn't make any sense.

There was no time to ponder the question because she had hardly gotten to her feet when she heard the door chimes.

She frowned as she left the room and went down the hall. It was now almost ten and she was alone here with Billy. When she reached the door she paused to glance through the peep-hole and then she bit her lower lip in consternation before she un-latched the door. It was Carla Bellamy. Sara would have liked to have ignored the summons, but since the house lights were on, it would appear strange if no one answered the door.

Carla gasped with surprise when she saw Sara. "What are you doing answering the door *here?*" she asked pointedly as she stepped into the hall without waiting for an invitation.

She was dressed casually in a pale pink skirt and blouse. Although the clothes were informal, she looked as though she had just stepped off a modeling platform. By contrast, Sara felt decidedly grubby in her Levis and cotton shirt, but unconsciously, she squared her shoulders and held her chin up proudly as she closed the door behind her unwanted guest.

"I'm staying here a few days with Billy," she answered briefly.

"Staying here?" Carla asked incredulously, be-fore demanding, "Where's Doug?"

"He's away on business," Sara explained in a calm voice. "Vernon's mother died this morning and he and Kate left this afternoon for Alabama. Kate asked me to stay with Billy until Doug returns."

Displeasure flashed in Carla's eyes. "The servants had no business taking it upon themselves to place you in charge here," she declared. "Doug's wishes should have been consulted."

"Perhaps," Sara agreed, "but there wasn't time. Kate needed someone right away."

"What if the people in Lucky hear about this?" Carla pointed out in a hostile voice. "How will it make you look, a single woman staying in Doug's house?"

Sara's amusement vied with her anger and sud-denly she threw back her head and laughed. "You've *got* to be kidding!" she gasped when she finally caught her breath. "In this day and age nobody would bat an eyelash! Besides, even if they did, Doug isn't here, so what could people gossip about?" She sobered as her amusement faded and then she leveled a frankly assessing gaze upon the other woman's face. "Anyway," she added, suddenly tired of beating around bushes, "who's reputation are you concerned about, Carla? Mine? Doug's? Or is it that you're afraid if people find out I'm here it will leave a little egg on *your* face?"

Sara was totally unprepared for what happened next. With the swiftness of a rattler's strike, Carla slapped her, then stepped back to glare at her with vicious hatred.

"You go ahead and stay here and play nursemaid to the boy," she said in a low, shaking voice, "but remember this! Doug belongs to me. So if he's your aim, you're completely wasting your time. He's in love with me!" Turning quickly on her heels, she went to the door and let herself out.

Carla's heated words returned to torment Sara throughout the following day. "He belongs to me," she had said. "He loves me." And sadly, Sara believed her. After all, Carla had once been his fiancée and certainly since her return, the two of then seemed quite intimate again. Sara supposed the intervening years had mellowed both of them. Doug was now able to forgive Carla for walking out on him and Carla was able to adjust to the reality of Billy's permanent position in Doug's life. So really it was just a matter of time until they set a wedding date. And that, Sara knew, was just an added reason for her to return to California as soon as possible. She would not want to be here when that happened.

Doug had mentioned once that he had wanted to ask her to be his wife, but she was certain now that it had been a lie. He had only said it in anger. That last night she had seen him, the night at the Country

Club, he had once again seemed to want her. But when Carla had arrived, he had changed abruptly. Doug, she thought bitterly, wanted too much. Admittedly, he was attracted to her, wanted to make love to her, maybe even to keep her on the side as his playmate and mistress if she were so obliging. But when he married it would be to the woman he had always loved—Carla.

The day was a busy one and Sara was glad to have a lot to do. She needed to keep her mind off the ugly scene with Carla and off the puzzling find of those records in Doug's study, as well. She prepared breakfast and shortly afterward, Wayne arrived for Billy's lessons. While they were occupied in the study, Sara found Kate's vacuum cleaner and did the upstairs rooms. Then there was lunch, which Wayne shared with them and soon after that, Beth arrived.

Sara noted what Kate had already pointed out, that Wayne and Beth were scrupulously careful to speak little to one another and then with only the barest polite civility. Although both of them seemed miserable and unnaturally grim, Sara was too wrapped up in her own unhappiness to scarcely care.

Later in the afternoon, once they were alone, Billy and Sara went outside. While Billy played with Rocky, Sara went to the barn to attend to the horses.

When she returned it was to find Billy rolling around on the patio with an excited, barking Rocky.

"Who's winning the wrestling match?" she asked with a smile.

"Rocky," Billy laughed. "He's trying to chew off my ear." He shoved the dog's face away from his and then struggled to sit up with his legs straight out in front of him. "Okay, boy, that's enough. Sit!"

Rocky wagged his golden-tan tail and obeyed. His tongue lolled out as he breathed heavily.

"Need some help getting up?" Sara offered,

throwing a meaningful glance at the abandoned wheelchair.

"Nope, I can do it myself," Billy answered. "Just shove the chair over here where I can reach it."

Sara complied, then said, "I'm going inside to get a Coke. Want one?"

Billy nodded as he pulled the chair into position and began levering himself up with his arms.

Sara hesitated an instant, ready to help if it was needed, but when Billy turned to glare at her, she quickly went inside the house. Obviously he was sensitive about people helping him do things he wanted to do independently.

"Gutsy kid," she mumbled to herself as she opened two Cokes, poured the dark liquid into glasses and added ice cubes.

She was just about to pick up the glasses and head back outside when she heard a scuffling noise from the front hall. She frowned, listening. Beth and Wayne had both long since gone and she had thought she had locked the front door. Warily, she went toward the hall door.

Doug was standing in the hall, glancing through his mail that had been stacked on a table there. At his feet were his bags. His suit coat was tossed across the table and his shoulders, beneath the white shirt seemed to be hunched as though he were exhausted.

Sara must have made some sound because suddenly he turned his head and looked in her direction. A surprised look flashed across his face and remembering he had no knowledge of what had happened, she went forward at once, saying with a slight catch in her throat, "I suppose you must be wondering what I'm doing here."

Doug's mouth gimaced into a tiny smile. "It doesn't matter why," he said softly. "It's just nice that you are."

Sara inhaled deeply. Whenever Doug was like this, it was hard to keep up a guard against him. She could feel the old magnetic pull drawing her senses toward him. She longed for nothing so much as to smooth away the lines of fatigue from his face, to watch his dark bleary eyes light up for her. The desire to touch him was so strong that she put her hands behind her and clasped them tightly together.

"I . . . we weren't expecting you back until next week," she said as matter-of-factly as she could.

Doug tossed the mail back onto the table, shrugged his shoulders carelessly and said, "I decided to cut the trip short." He crossed the remaining space between them until they were standing only inches apart. "Why are you here? Did you come to visit Kate and Billy?"

"Not exactly." Quickly, Sara explained about Vernon's mother. "So," she ended, "Kate asked me to stay with Billy until you returned and could find someone else to suit you. I'm afraid they don't know when they'll be coming back, but Vernon said it would be as soon as possible and that he'll be in touch with you."

Doug smiled again, but now Sara could see that the smile did not quite reach his eyes, that his face was abnormally colorless. There was a drawn, pinched look around his mouth. "You suit me fine," he said steadily. "Thank you for taking over on such short notice."

Sara waved the words away almost impatiently as she studied him more closely. "Are you feeling all right, Doug?"

"Fine," he answered swiftly. "Or maybe just a little tired," he amended. "Got any coffee?"

"No. I was just pouring Cokes for Billy and myself, but I'll make some for you." She turned and began walking back toward the kitchen.

"Don't bother," Doug said from just behind her

as he followed her. "I'd just as soon have something cold myself."

Billy had come inside by the time they entered the kitchen and he greeted Doug with a war-whoop of welcome. "How come you're back so early?"

Doug sank heavily into one of the kitchen chairs. "It was just a spur of the moment decision. Why didn't you or Sara telephone me about what happened? I left the hotel number with Kate."

"We talked it over," Billy answered before Sara could, "and we decided not to bother you. There wasn't anything you could do and besides, Sara and I had things under control here."

"I'm sure of it," Doug replied as he accepted the Coke Sara handed him. Turning to her, he asked, "What about flowers? If I had known I—"

Sara joined him at the table. "I wired a wreath from you and Billy and a separate one from me."

"You do have things well in hand," he said gratefully. "Thanks." He drained his glass and shoved back his chair. "Guess I'll go unpack and take a shower."

He left the room and shortly afterward Billy went outside again to feed Rocky. Left alone, Sara was uncertain whether Doug expected her to leave immediately now that he was home or to stay through dinner. But she did not have the nerve to seek him out in his bedroom to find out and she would have felt silly sending Billy to ask. So when Doug did not return a half hour later, she decided to go ahead and prepare dinner. After all, they had to eat, Doug was tired from his trip and surely wouldn't want to bother with it himself. And if it was left up to Billy, there would be the inevitable hot dogs again.

She had a chicken baking in the oven, a rice and almond dish on top of the stove and was tossing a salad when Billy returned almost an hour later.

"What've you been up to?" she asked. Then she

happened to turn and get a glimpse of him. His face boasted a streak of red paint while more of it adorned his shirt and hands. "Billy!" she exclaimed. "What are you trying to do, become a fire engine?"

Billy grinned a bit shamefacedly as he glanced down at his hands. "Vernon and I built a dog house for Rocky and I wanted to have it painted before he comes home. I guess," he said in a master understatement, "I sorta got some on me, too."

"By the looks of you, I doubt any got on the dog house," Sara told him. "Dinner's nearly ready," she added, "so how about you trying to wash away some of the warpaint and then calling Doug for me?"

"Sure." Billy whirled the chair around and rolled toward the hall. "Whatever you've got smells good and I'm starved!"

The dinner was on the table when Billy came back, much cleaner, even though there was still a dab of red paint under his chin. "J.D.'s asleep," he announced, "and when I tried to wake him he started tossing around and mumbling strange things and his face is kinda red."

"Sure you didn't smear paint on him?" Sara teased to hide the worry that suddenly gripped her. "Go ahead and serve your plate, Billy. Maybe I'd better check on him."

Billy's observations had been accurate, Sara discovered when she reluctantly entered Doug's bedroom, which was located just behind the study. Still fully dressed, Doug tossed about restlessly on the bed and his face, which had been pale earlier, was now darkly flushed.

Sara stretched out a hand and touched his forehead. He was definitely feverish. She caught her lower lip between her teeth and gazed down at him in consternation. Then she went into his bathroom, opened the medicine chest and began rummaging through it.

142

When she returned, she had to shake him awake. Doug groaned but at last he opened his glazed eyes and focused them on her. "What is it?" he mumbled. "What's the matter?"

"You're burning up with fever," she said. "Why didn't you tell me earlier that you were ill?"

"I'll be okay," he said obstinately. "I just needed a nap, that's all." He sat up on the edge of the bed.

Sara shook the thermometer and ordered, "Put this in your mouth. Then I'll give you some aspirin before I go call Royce."

"Don't need Royce," Doug muttered. "A couple of aspirins will fix me up."

His temperature was slightly above a hundred and three. Sara saw that Doug swallowed the aspirins then asked, "What are your symptoms? And how long have you been feeling this way?"

"Started yesterday," he said as he nursed his brow with his fingers. "I ache all over, my throat hurts and I'm either too hot or too cold." His voice sounded plaintive, like a small boy's.

"Sounds like the flu," Sara said. "Get undressed and into bed properly while I call Royce. I'll be back in a little while with some fruit juice. Do you want any dinner?"

Doug managed a wobbly grin. "No dinner . . . but if you want to stay and help me undress, I'd be—"

Sara made a face at him. "You're not as sick as I thought," she said tartly. "Or else you're delirious." She turned and marched smartly from the room.

When she got Royce on the phone he agreed that it sounded like a virus and he promised to have the drug store in Lucky deliver the needed antibiotics.

There was no question now of Sara's returning to the cabin that night. She could hardly leave Billy alone to cope with Doug's illness.

Nor was there any question of it during the next

couple of days. Doug alternated between alert irritability and irrational feverishness. Sara had her hands full with him and scarcely even noticed the comings and goings of Beth and Wayne. If she wasn't trying to get his medication or juices down Doug, she was preparing soups she hoped would tempt him. At other times she was busy changing his perspiration-soaked sheets or trying to convince him that he was too ill to dress and go to the office.

The latter was fast becoming a major argument between them and Billy was an enormous help to Sara in seeing that Doug did not attempt it. Whenever she was busy in another part of the house, he kept an eye on Doug, checking every few minutes to see whether he was sleeping or trying to get dressed.

The second night was the worst. Doug's fever climbed frighteningly and Sara tried unsuccessfully to reach Royce. In the end, she sat in Doug's room all night, sponging his hot face with a cold cloth and trying to straighten out the shambles he was making of his bed as he tossed and turned.

During the night he mumbled a great deal, mostly about business matters. Sometimes he mentioned Vernon's name, or in his dream-reality, told Billy to do something. Sara could make no sense of any of it, but it bothered her to hear him. She knew he could not be resting comfortably.

And then she was startled to hear him say "Sheila." She had been curled up in a chair, but the name brought her bolt upright and she stared at him in blank amazement. She listened attentively, but he did not repeat the name again and she was left in frustrated bewilderment, wondering if he had been speaking of her.

On the third day, the worst of Doug's illness seemed to be over. He was still pale and wan, was running a low-grade fever off and on, but it was apparent that he was definitely on the mend. He had an appetite and even sat up that evening for a couple of hours watching television.

Two days later he was fully recovered. Sara was in the kitchen, starting breakfast, when he walked in briskly, dressed neatly in dark brown trousers and a tan shirt. He was freshly showered and his hair glistened with droplets of water.

"Morning," he greeted as he came to stand beside her at the counter where she was slicing ham. "You look very fetching," he said approvingly as his gaze roamed over her belted white robe and then traveled up to her slender throat, her face and even up to her hair which was tied back with a pale blue ribbon. Impulsively, he reached out and touched a lock of her hair. "You also look very much at home here. We could almost be married, couldn't we . . . the way you've taken care of me and my home this past week?" His voice was soft and suggestive.

Warily, like an animal trying to avoid a trap, Sara moved sharply away from him, causing a sudden frown to crease his forehead. This time she wasn't falling for his bait. Too many times Doug had played with her, enticing her and then ending up hurting her. The past few days had been difficult, taking care of him, fighting her love for him. But she had her emotions under tight control and now she was not going to loosen the bonds on them. "We're not married, however," she said almost curtly, "and now that you're well, perhaps I ought to return to the cabin today."

"I'd appreciate it if you'd stay until Kate comes back," he said in a flat, unemotional voice which was totally unlike the flirtatious one he had used only a moment ago. "I need to get back to the office and Billy can't stay here alone. I'd be willing to pay you if—"

Sara shook her head vigorously. Her eyes met his

briefly and then she glanced down once more at the knife in her hand. "No . . . no pay. I'll stay, of course, as long as Billy needs me."

Without warning, Doug grabbed her arm and jerked her around to face him. "In other words, it's only Billy you care about?" He asked in a rigid voice. "Not me?"

Sara nodded, pressing her trembling lips tightly together.

"What," Doug demanded, still in that hard, inflexible voice, "have I ever done to make you hate me so much?"

Sara turned away. "I don't trust you," she said hollowly. "Let's just say it's one of those odd personality quirks people sometimes have. We needn't try to analyze it." She laid the knife on the counter, picked up the bowl of pancake batter she had mixed previously and was about to pour some of it onto the griddle when Doug jerked her arm again, causing her to spill some of the batter on the floor. "Thunderation and tarnation!" she exclaimed in dismay. "Now look what you made me do!"

She set the bowl back onto the counter, reached for some paper towels to wipe up the mess. But she suddenly found herself gripped by the shoulders and then she was being roughly shaken.

Doug's face, close to hers, was fierce and menacing like an enraged mountain lion. "You're Sheila Starr!" he spat out violently. "You deceitful, spiteful little witch! You came here deliberately to make a fool of me, didn't you . . . to try to make me fall in love with you so you could score me off for what happened between us before!"

Chapter Eight

The intensity of Doug's anger was terrifying. His face was suffused with dark color and his black eyes, narrowed to mere slits, glittered pure danger. His stance was rigid and his fists were knotted at his sides.

The atmosphere was suddenly charged with deadly currents of hostility and with an instinctive wariness, Sara backed away until the safety of several feet divided them. Her own face had gone pale until it was almost as white as her robe. Only her eyes glowed with color—a blue hazed with gray, the pupils enlarged by fear and disbelief.

"It isn't true," she whispered shakily. "I never even knew you were here."

A contemptuous scorn curled Doug's hard mouth. "Don't attempt to play me for an even bigger fool!" he snarled. "It's all perfectly clear to me now . . . the kitten softness alternating with cold rejection. You came to try to make me fall in love with you, to get me to ask you to marry me just so you could have the pleasure of turning me down! That night I carried you to your bedroom and at the last minute you called a halt . . . it was all for fun, wasn't it? What a laugh you must have had at my expense!" Sharply, he turned his back to her and the crash of his fist on the table reverberated through the room.

In dismay, Sara stared at the lean, solid width of

his back. She longed to go to him, to touch him, to somehow wipe away the stiff anger and hurt. But she did not dare. His bitterness was far too great. She had thought he was angry that night three years ago, but it had been nothing compared to the violence of his rage now. This was like a fire devouring all that stood in its relentless path.

"It isn't true," she repeated and she hated the betraying quiver in her voice. "Honest, Doug, when I came here it was only to find a place to stay where I could become well again. I had no idea you owned the cabin or lived nearby yourself. I was completely shocked that first night when you came to the door."

"Sure," he snapped, half turning to glare at her. "That explains everything. If that's true, then when I said you looked familiar, why didn't you admit who you really were? Why did you feed me a line the next day about being a dress shop clerk?" His voice had been sarcastic and now he shook his head, utterly rejecting her words. "You were very careful that I shouldn't know who you really were." Now he ran a restless hand across his forehead. "Maybe I can understand your urge for revenge, but I sure as hell can't understand Agnes being a part of it and helping you to set me up for the kill. I had thought she was my friend."

"She is," Sara insisted. "I swear it, Doug. Agnes doesn't know a thing about us . . . about . . ." her voice hesitated, "about our prior relationship. She has no idea that we met at her party. When I wanted a place to stay in the mountains she simply contacted you because she must have known you owned a cabin. It's as simple as that . . . a coincidence, nothing more."

"Is it?" he asked icily. "Then why all the secrecy about your real identity? Your face has haunted me and so has your voice, but fool that I was I never connected either with the famous Sheila Starr. Why

148

did you lie, Sara . . . if you hadn't had it all planned out in advance? You signed the lease as Sara Scott."

"That's my real name," Sara defended herself, "but as to why I didn't tell you the truth," she gave her head a tiny shake, "I simply can't explain it to you."

Doug's eyes were as cold as his voice, like two rain-washed black stones. "You mean you won't explain."

She nodded and her chin jutted out stubbornly as she met his gaze unflinchingly. "That's right," she said flatly, "I won't." Now her anger matched his. Obviously Doug was going to think the worst of her no matter what she said, so attempting to convince him of her sincerity was fruitless. He would never believe she had not come here with the intention of tricking him. She could not, and would not, explain the real truth about why she had shielded her identity—that she had dreaded his pity for the shell of her old self that she now was, that she had also feared his scorn as well. But never in her wildest imagination had she thought that he might believe she had come for revenge.

"What's for breakfast?" A voice asked from the doorway. And then it added, "Yuk, what a mess! What's all that junk on the floor?"

Sara glanced across the room to see Billy, dressed in faded cut off jeans and a yellow T-shirt, leaning on his crutches. On his face was an expression of disgust as he stared at the mess.

Sara, released at last from the powerful itensity of Doug's bitter anger, swung into action. She reached for the paper towels and bent down to the floor. "I'm afraid that *was* our breakfast," she said over her shoulder to the boy. "I'll have it cleaned up in a jiffy, though, and then I'll get things going."

A dark brown hand suddenly covered hers and Sara lifted her surprised eyes to meet Doug's. He had stooped down too, and their faces were close. A warning light flickered in his eyes as though he were telling her to behave normally, just as though nothing had occurred.

"I'll clean this up," he said quietly in a level voice. "You go ahead and get started with the food."

"Thank you." Sara nodded and quickly got to her feet and turned toward the counter. The pressure of his hand on hers, coming so soon after the storm between them, had left her shaken and breathless and she was glad to put a little distance between them. The worst—the very worst thing that could happen would be if Doug ever read the real truth in her eyes—that she loved him. As much as he now hated her, it would be disastrous. Once again he would cruelly reject her, just the same as he had done that dreadful night they had been together in California. She knew she could never survive such an occurrence a second time. She was even more defenseless and vulnerable now and the guard she had kept these past few months would have to be rigidly maintained. Doug, believing she had come here only to make a fool of him, would not only not believe the truth but even if he should, he would be contemptuous of it.

Somehow the two of them carried off the illusion that all was well between them during breakfast. For Billy's sake they made conversation, but it was a strain and Sara, who had never felt less like eating in her life, struggled to force down her food.

Apparently they succeeded in hiding the hostility that had flared between them, because Billy chattered away during the meal in his normal enthusiastic way and seemed not to notice anything amiss. Even so, Sara felt only vast relief when the boy at last left the table and went outside to feed his dog.

An awkward silence settled between Doug and Sara as soon as Billy was gone. She was acutely aware of him sitting directly across the table from her, but she did not have the courage to look up at him. Instead, she pushed back her chair, got up and went over to the stove where she poured herself a second cup of coffee. But instead of returning to the table, she stood self-consciously and stared unseeingly out the window over the sink.

Unaware that Doug had left the table and come to stand just behind her, Sara stiffened when he spoke. "I'm sure," he said in a flat, unemotional tone, "the last thing you want to do is to continue staying here in my house now. But all the same, I'd appreciate it if you would stay until Kate comes back. I'll stay out of your way as much as possible, of course. If you want to go now, I'll understand and make some other sort of arrangements about taking care of Billy while I'm away at the office."

Hot tears scalded Sara's eyes and she was glad her back was to Doug so that he could not see how much his words hurt. What he was really saying, of course, was that he wanted her to leave as quickly as possible so that he would never have to see her again. And, she thought sadly, it would be best for the both of them if she did go away right now. It would be best to sever their relationship now, in one abrupt slice that while painful, would be over and done with in an instant. She could begin packing, make arrangements to have the bulk of her things sent by truck and set out in her car for California this very day.

She was just about to say that she would go at once, as soon as he could make his other arrangements for Billy, when she happened to glimpse the boy outside the window, slowly making his way on his crutches as he went toward the barn to visit the horses. Then she knew she couldn't do it. The "other arrangements" Doug spoke of was in all likelihood Carla and she could not do that to Billy. She already knew he disliked Carla and Carla herself had made no bones about her aversion to caring for the boy when she had come here several nights ago. Sara had grown to love Billy and because she did, she could not subject him to Carla's indifferent care.

With a deep sigh, she spoke in a low voice while her back was still turned to Doug. "I'll stay until Kate comes back."

"Thank you," came the quiet reply. Then Doug added, "Well, I'd better head on to the office. Since I've been away over a week, I'm sure the work has piled up." She heard his footsteps as he crossed the room toward the door, heard them come to a halt and then he added in an oddly strained voice, "By the way, despite the way things are between us, I am grateful for the care you've given me these past few days while I was ill as well as the care you've given to Billy."

Sara nodded her head up and down and swallowed hard. "You're welcome," she said huskily. "I was happy to do it."

She braved herself to turn at last and looked at him. For an instant, time was suspended as they gazed at one another, and then Doug nodded in a business-like fashion and went briskly from the room.

In Sara's opinion Doug was still not quite strong enough for the long drive into Denver and a hard day's work even though he was far better than he had been yesterday. But after the ugly words between them she had not dared to risk suggesting that he spend one more day at home before resuming his normal activities. He might have gotten the wrong idea and in some way decided that she wanted him to stay at home on her account, so she allowed him to leave without a word of protest. If he came down with a relapse he just would and there was nothing she could do to prevent it.

Somehow the day passed. Sara kept busy with household chores while Billy had his regular sessions with Wayne and Beth. Then it was suddenly time to prepare their evening meal.

Sara was tense as she cooked a roast and baked potatoes and a banana pudding for their dessert. What sort of mood would Doug be in when he came home? Would the mask of peace still be in place for Billy's benefit or would there be open hostilities again? Until Kate came back to take over she would constantly be walking a tightrope where Doug was concerned. As she shoved the roast into the oven, Sara desperately wished that Kate would walk through the door at that very moment so that she would be free to leave.

No such miracle occurred, however, by the time the dinner was finished at last and was warming in the oven. Sara threw a quick glance at the kitchen clock and decided she had time for a quick shower and a change of clothes before Doug was expected back.

A few minutes later, refreshed from her shower and dressed in a neat but unpretentious navy blue skirt and blouse, Sara stopped by Billy's room before going back downstairs. She found him busily at work on a model airplane.

"Dinner's ready and I'm not sure whether Doug will be home soon or not. If you want to eat now, I'll fix your plate."

Billy shook his head as he bent his head low over a wing. "I'll wait and eat when you and J.D. do," he said absently. "I want to get this piece done first anyway."

"Sure." Sara left his room and went briskly toward the stairs. She would just check to make sure the dinner was all right and then watch the evening news on television until Doug came.

She had visualized Doug angry or Doug polite

whenever he did arrive, and most of all she had visualized him there alone with Billy and her. But as she descended the stairs she received an unwelcome surprise. Doug stood in the entrance hall and at his side stood Carla Bellamy.

One glance at Carla's lovely elegance quickly erased any satisfaction Sara might have had up to that point about her own appearance. Carla, dressed in cream-colored slacks and a matching sweater knit top that was edged with bulky fringe, looked as though she were posing for a fashion magazine. Her dark hair, swept back to reveal the delicate bone structure of her face, was luxuriously beautiful and her makeup was flawless. Her wine-colored lips were parted in a smile.

"Hello," she greeted pleasantly, just as though they were the best of friends. "I hope Doug is paying you enough for all the hard work you've been doing. I'm sure you aren't used to all the responsibility a young boy and a house this size entails."

"I'm just fine," Sara replied evenly as she knotted her hands behind her. She was seething at Carla's reference to pay and knew it had been done deliberately as a put-down but she would have died before giving the other woman the satisfaction of knowing it rankled her. What was astounding was that Carla was able to carry off the pretense of care and friendliness after the scene between them the last time they had met. Certainly from her behavior just now, Doug could never possibly guess that there had ever been any dispute between them.

"Sara has handled things magnificently," Doug said, unexpectedly coming to her defense, "without expecting pay at all. In addition to everything else, the past few days she's had to contend with me while I was ill."

"You've been ill?" Carla asked in swift surprise.

"You should have called me, Doug. I would have come to take care of you so that Sara wouldn't have had to worry."

Doug's lips twisted into a wry smile. "Somehow I just can't visualize you playing nurse, Carla, bullying me into swallowing pills and juices and physically restraining me from going to the office. Sara, I've discovered, can be very stern when she wants." His eyes seemed soft as they sought and found Sara's. But all at once, as though he recalled the scene between them that morning, his black eyes hardened, the smile faded from his lips and he said in an entirely different voice, "However, I'm fully recovered now and Carla and I are going out to dinner tonight. You and Billy will be all right here alone?"

"Of course," Sara said stiffly. "You mustn't worry about us." Her face became a frozen mask that effectively hid her emotions. If Doug wanted to hurt her, wanted to show her just how unimportant she was to him, he was doing an excellent job of it by bringing Carla here tonight in order to show her where his real interest lay. But Sara's pride was too strong to permit him to see the truth.

It was an hour before the mask was allowed to crumble. Once Doug and Carla were gone, Sara and Billy shared dinner together. Just as it had been that morning, she found it difficult to manage more than a few bites.

As soon as they had finished eating, Billy decided to go upstairs for his bath and then planned to watch a movie on television in his bedroom. Sara was secretly relieved that for the remainder of the evening she would be entirely alone. She didn't know how much longer she would have been able to maintain her front of calm equanimity.

There was no question of how much Doug hated her. True, during the past couple of months he had been drawn to her physically just as he had been several years ago. But there was no deeper emotion on his part. He might, at times, have thought he loved her, but it wasn't true. Whatever his attraction to her, it had not been able to survive the blow his pride had been dealt this morning when he had realized who she really was. He believed she had come here to deliberately make a fool of him, and why not? It was, after all, what he had done once to her. And now that he knew the truth, he was done with her for good. He had not wanted her on a permanent basis before and he didn't now.

Sara's mouth curled into a bitter smile as she mounted the stairs and entered her bedroom. Permanent basis, indeed! What a laugh! That was something Doug had never wanted with her. He had wanted her to be his mistress, his lover. When it came to marriage, she had never even been in the running. That prize had always been reserved for Carla.

Perhaps they would even become formally engaged this very night, Sara thought. Absently, she began to undress, letting her clothes fall into a crumpled heap at her feet. Certainly, her mind trooped on relentlessly, Carla had seemed very confident and sure of herself this evening and Doug had appeared most receptive to her smiles. Carla's slender hand had been tucked possessively around Doug's arm as they had left and Doug had not seemed to mind in the least.

As she slid a silky nightgown over her head, Sara pictured the two of them together, heads close as they whispered intimate words to one another— Doug's mouth claiming the softness of Carla's red lips, their bodies pressed tightly together.

She squeezed her eyes shut just as though the action would banish the torturing vision that played across the screen of her mind. But it did not go away and after an instant, she opened them again, crossed to the dresser and picked up her hairbrush.

Vigorously, she attacked her hair, brushing it so hard that sudden tears smarted in her eyes. Then, just as abruptly, the hairbrush fell with a clatter from her limp hand onto the dresser. In defeat, Sara gazed at her reflection in the mirror. Her eyes held a haunted expression that she could not bear to see and at once she turned away. The ache of hopeless love weighted down her heart like a heavy boulder pressing the very air from her lungs.

It was late—very late, when she finally fell into an exhausted sleep and until she did, she was keenly aware that Doug had not returned home.

When she went downstairs the next morning, Billy was already in the kitchen, eating cold cereal. The aroma of fresh coffee permeated the room.

"Did you make the coffee?" Sara asked in mild surprise.

Billy shook his head and swallowed some orange juice before answering. "J.D. did. He just left for the office."

"Oh, I see," Sara said quietly as she went to fill a coffee cup for herself. Doug was being extremely careful to stay out of her way. A deep depression settled heavily on her shoulders. Obviously he could not stand to be in her company even for a moment.

A few minutes later Wayne arrived and Billy vanished into the study with him. Sara listlessly cleaned the kitchen, not even remembering she had not eaten any breakfast herself. Her one desire now was for Kate to come back so that she could leave. The situation with Doug was intolerable and she didn't know how much longer she could endure being in his home while he did everything in his power to avoid even the slightest contact with her.

At midmorning, Beth telephoned. "Hi, Sara," she said. "Thought I'd better let you know not to expect me today."

"Why?" Sara asked curiously. "Have you caught Doug's virus?"

"No. I've had a slight accident with my car. A fender-bender only," she added hastily, "and I'm not hurt. Just mad. This idiot came out of a shopping center and plowed into me without even looking at where he was going. Anyway, my car's been towed off to a garage and I'm sitting in my doctor's waiting room."

"I thought you said you weren't hurt!" Sara exclaimed.

"I'm not except for a bruise or two, honestly," Beth insisted. "It's just that my boss ordered me to get a checkup just to make sure and then I'm supposed to go home and rest for the remainder of the day."

"I heartily approve of your boss," Sara commented, "so you just do exactly what he says. Do you think you'll be here tomorrow?"

"Yes. The office will provide me with another car while mine's being repaired. I'll be there for sure tomorrow."

"All right, then," Sara said. "Pamper yourself like crazy this afternoon. Bye."

A half hour later, Sara was vacuuming the living room carpet when she happened to glance up and see Wayne and Billy entering the room. She switched off the vacuum and abruptly the loud noise ceased. "You guys finished with lessons already?" she asked.

"Yep," Billy replied with a self-satisfied look on his face. "I had to take my final English test and I made a ninety-four!"

"That's great!" Sara ruffled Billy's hair with a

fond gesture. "When Kate comes back she's going to be very proud of you, and so am I!"

Wayne had been smiling, too, but now he frowned. "I hope Kate and Vernon get back before I leave at the end of the week. I'd hate to leave without saying goodbye to them."

"They'll be sorry if that happens, too," Sara said. Then she glanced down at Billy again. "By the way, pal, you're getting off easy this afternoon. Beth can't come today."

"You mean I get the whole afternoon off?"

Sara nodded. "That's right."

"Then can I call Larry and see if he can come spend the afternoon with me?"

Sara smiled. "Why not?"

As though he were afraid to allow her time to change her mind, Billy immediately wheeled his chair from the room. An amused smile lingered on Sara's lips as she returned her attention to Wayne. "I'm about to make some ham sandwiches for lunch," she told him. "Would you like to stay and join us?"

"Thanks," Wayne answered. "I believe I will. My cupboard is practically bare. I'm letting my supply run down since I'll be leaving soon." As Sara turned toward the door, he followed, asking, "Why isn't Beth coming today?"

Sara tossed her reply over her shoulder. "She was involved in a car accident."

"What?" The one word was explosive.

Sara stopped and when she turned fully to really look at Wayne, she saw that his face had gone a pasty white. Instantly, her hand went out to give his arm a reassuring squeeze. "She's all right," she said quickly. "Just a bruise or two."

Beneath her hand, Wayne's arm was suddenly trembling. He groaned and lifted his other hand to brush across his face. Anxiety strained his voice. "Are you sure she's all right? Is she in the hospital?"

"No. She called from her doctor's office where she had gone for a checkup and then she was going back to her apartment to rest."

Wayne went suddenly still and was silent for a long moment before he said quietly, "I love that girl, you know."

"Do you?" Sara asked skeptically. "Then why are you going away and leaving her here? Seems to me if you really loved her you'd marry her and take her with you. She's a wonderful person, Wayne. How long do you think it will be before some other smart man realizes that?"

"You don't understand, Sara," Wayne said morosely. "I'm going back to a lot of family and financial problems. I want nothing more than to marry Beth, but right now I don't have a thing worth offering to her."

"You have yourself," Sara said quietly. "If you really love her, don't you think you should at least give her the choice of sharing the bad times as well as the good? Do you think so little of her character that you don't believe she would stick it out unless things were rosy all the time?"

Chagrined, Wayne glared down at his feet, but at last he lifted his head and gave Sara a wry grin. "You don't pull any punches, do you?" He asked in an embarrassed voice.

Sara gave him an answering grin. "Well, Beth is my friend and it makes me angry for you to believe she's as shallow as all that."

"I don't," Wayne said stoutly. "It's only that I was trying to protect her. I just don't think it's fair that she should start out a marriage burdened with other people's troubles."

"And is it fair to break her heart?"

Wayne's gaze was thoughtful as it met hers. Then,

without warning, Sara was enveloped in a bear hug. "Forget the sandwiches," he told her with a throaty laugh. "There's an errand I just remembered I have to attend to . . . and it's urgent."

Sara laughed too and called to his swiftly retreating back, "Good luck!"

But as soon as Wayne was gone, her smile faded. She hoped fervently that things would work out for the other couple, but she was still confronted with her own problem and she could see no happy ending in her own future.

The following day, with glowing smiles, Beth and Wayne announced they were now planning a wedding. Wayne was still leaving in a matter of days, but would be returning in a month's time to claim his bride. Sara was glad for them, Billy, openly scornful about all that "love junk" as he termed it, while Doug was noncommittal outside of offering the couple his congratulations. His gaze was dark and somber as it met Sara's and she quickly glanced away, wishing that the entire subject of love and marriage could have been avoided while she was in Doug's presence.

On the surface, things seemed calm enough during the next couple of days. Sara's encounters with Doug were few and brief and both of them were able to maintain a calm, polite truce. Most of Sara's time was spent with Billy, who, she discovered, in spite of his handicap, had more energy than three boys. Together they played with Rocky, went on picnic walks and tended the horses. Billy wanted to go horseback riding, but here Sara balked. She had never been at ease on a horse's back and no persuasion of Billy's was about to change her mind. In the end, they compromised on a drive into Denver one afternoon and went to a movie.

Late that evening, after Billy had already gone to

sleep, Sara decided to take a bath and shampoo her hair. As usual, Doug was not home and she had spent most of the evening in her bedroom with the radio going while she flipped through a couple of fashion magazines she had picked up in town.

She didn't bother turning off the radio as she left her room and went down the hall to the bathroom.

When she had finished her shower and was toweling dry, she realized she had left her blow dryer in the bedroom. Since she knew Billy was sound asleep in his room with his door closed, she didn't bother with her robe. She simply wrapped the thick bath towel around her, sarong fashion and hurried out into the hall.

The sight of Doug brought her up short. He was standing in the hall before her opened bedroom door. A shaft of light spilled from the doorway, illuminating his face so that his features were thrown into sharp relief.

"What . . . are you doing up here?" Sara's mouth felt cottony.

"I came to check on the noise I heard downstairs . . . your radio, apparently. I thought maybe it was Billy still awake with the TV going. Do you usually run around like that?" His voice held a grim, forbidding note.

Sara's cheeks scalded and she inched past him into her room, careful to keep a tight grip on the towel that suddenly seemed woefully inadequate as a covering.

"I forgot my hair dryer, that's all," she said defensively, "and I knew Billy was asleep. I never dreamed you were even in the house, much less that you would come up here."

Doug moved so swiftly that she had no time to realize what was happening. In one movement he was inside the room with her, had kicked the door shut behind him and she was crushed against his rock-hard chest. She saw a flicker of fire in his eyes just before his head descended and his mouth claimed hers.

For one stunned instant, Sara did not move. She felt his fingers threading through the strands of her wet hair and then one hand slid down her back, pressing her even closer to his lean, solid frame. All at once, molten lava burned its way through her veins and her hand moved upward of its own volition to slide into the opened neck of his shirt.

His probing fingers tugged at the towel and a moment later, it dropped to the floor. Doug's hands ran gently up over her breasts, down to her waist and hips and then traveled slowly up again, leaving a trail of fire wherever they went.

"You're in my blood," he whispered huskily as his teeth nibbled playfully at an ear lobe, "and I can't seem to get you out. I want you, Sara . . . now."

Sara's entire body throbbed with her aching, unsatisfied desire. Her senses reeled at his every caress and she knew she could deny neither her needs nor his any longer. "I want you, too," she whispered back.

Doug gave a tiny, exultant laugh from deep in his throat as he scooped her up and carried her to the bed. Sara's hands crept up and began working the buttons loose from the buttonholes on his shirt.

Doug smiled, then bent over to possess her lips again. "Who's getting revenge on whom tonight, I wonder?" he murmured as his fingers tangled themselves in her hair once more.

His words were like a bucket of cold water thrown in her face. Sara's hands froze against his chest and then she was shoving him away. At the incredulous expression on his face, she flared, "You still believe that's why I came, don't you?"

Doug's eyes narrowed. "I know that it is, but what difference does it make? We both want each other now, tonight, and that's what matters."

"Is it?" Sara's voice trembled as she rolled off the bed. Suddenly conscious of her nudity, she grabbed a blanket from the foot of the bed and wrapped it around her. Only once she was covered did she have sufficient courage to look at Doug again.

"It wasn't enough three years ago," she reminded him with bitterness. "You wanted me then, too, until you became afraid that it might demand some sort of commitment from you. Well, I wasn't asking for a commitment then and I don't expect one now, either. No matter how much I may want you, I won't let you make love to me. It would make a complete mockery of the word when you still believe only the very worst of me." With an abrupt motion, she turned sharply away and added in a muffled voice, "Now . . . please get out of here!"

She did not see Doug again before she left his house for good with a silent vow to herself that she would never set foot inside it again. He was gone already the following morning when she got downstairs and near noon, Vernon and Kate arrived back at last. Sara welcomed them back with deep relief, prepared a light lunch for them while they unpacked and afterward packed her few clothes into her bag and returned to the cabin.

The stillness and quiet of it seemed strange after so many days away and Sara let the peace surround her and penetrate her consciousness as she slumped onto the sofa before the empty fireplace. She should, she knew, immediately take inventory, deciding what could be packed in the car for the drive to California and what could be sent by movers. But for the moment, she lacked the necessary energy. She was away from Doug and his house and just now, that was enough. Still, the sooner she made arrangements with a moving company about shipping her piano and other large belongings, the quicker she could leave here for good.

But before she had so much as lifted a finger toward doing any of those things, the telephone rang and it was Royce. "Hi," he said in a cheerful voice. "I've been instructed to call and tell you to expect a guest this weekend."

"Oh . . . who?"

"Agnes. She'll be flying in Saturday afternoon and will stay until Wednesday."

"Really?" Sara was astounded that Agnes would be making another trip here so soon after she had returned home, and then something else surprised her. "How come," she demanded suddenly, "the message is coming through you? Why didn't Agnes call me instead?"

Royce chuckled. "I'll tell you tonight if you'll come have dinner with me."

"Hmm, you sound very mysterious. Can't you tell me now?"

"Nope," Royce said firmly. "You have to come to dinner."

Sara laughed. "All right, meanie. I'll be there at seven."

When Royce opened the door for her that evening, Sara was immediately struck by a change in him. It was an intangible thing, an aura rather than anything physical. Years seemed to have dropped from him. His shoulders seemed straighter; there was a deeper light to his eyes and he appeared more relaxed than she had ever seen him.

"What's happened to you?" She asked as they walked into the living room together. "Did you just win a million dollars in a lottery or something?"

Royce grinned and to Sara's amazement, his face turned a dull shade of pink. "Is it that obvious?"

"That you're very satisfied about something?" Sara nodded. "Yes, it is, so how about letting me in on the secret."

"Agnes has consented to be my wife."

Sara's eyes widened. *My* Agnes?"

Royce chuckled from deep in his throat. "No," he corrected with pride. "My Agnes."

"How marvelous!" Sara exclaimed once the news had fully penetrated. "I knew all along you were perfect for each other, but I was afraid neither of you had the sense to see it for yourselves!" She teased. "Tell me, when and how did all this come about?"

"Sit down." Royce waved a hand toward the sofa as he moved toward the bar where he mixed them each a martini. "Last weekend I flew to L.A. and proposed. She's coming this weekend so we can work out the details of the date . . . probably in a month or two. She'll have to square away her business there, of course, before she can be free to move. She called last night to say she's going to sell out the agency to her chief assistant . . . a man named Rudy, I think."

Sara nodded, accepted her drink and sipped at it thoughtfully. She was delighted for her two friends, of course, but Agnes' new plans rather left her floundering. She could still go back to Los Angeles herself and let Rudy handle her, but it wouldn't be the same without Agnes there bullying her every step of the way.

Throughout dinner they talked of little except the upcoming wedding and when they returned to the living room with coffee afterward, Royce said, "By the way, Agnes mentioned something about the possibility of you singing at our wedding."

"You know who I am, then?" Sara asked quietly.

Royce nodded. "Agnes told me last week. I hope you don't mind. She did swear me to secrecy."

Sara shook her head. "No, I don't mind you knowing." In truth, it didn't seem to matter who knew anymore since she had decided at last to return to her career.

The door bell chimed and Royce excused himself to answer it. In only a moment, he returned with Doug following him.

"Have a seat, J.D. Would you like a drink or coffee?"

Doug drew up short at the sight of Sara, and seemed as startled by her presence as she was by his. Their gazes collided with the devastating impact of a tornado ripping into a slumbering town. Then, Doug's jaw became a wall of concrete while his eyes darkened into midnight black storm clouds.

"Nothing for me, thanks," he finally answered Royce. "I only stopped by to tell you that Billy and I are going camping this weekend and I was wondering if you'd like to come with us."

"Thanks, but I can't make it," Royce answered. "I've already got plans. Ask me again next trip, okay?"

"Sure thing." Doug's voice was clipped and abrupt. "I'd better be going. I'm sorry to have interrupted you." His frigid gaze once more raked across Sara before he turned and left the room.

Sara shivered. Doug had not spoken a single word to her, and yet the effects of his censorious gaze left her shaken just as much as if they had had a violent argument. She had already known that Doug hated her, but tonight she realized that he despised her as well.

Chapter Nine

Although it was mid-November, it looked and felt like spring. The water in the swimming pool sparkled beneath the bright golden sun and the grass and shrubs beyond the pool were a vivid green.

Sara sprawled in a lounge chair near the pool, her slender ankles crossed, eyes brooding as she occasionally took a sip of iced tea. She knew she should go inside the house and begin packing for the trip to Denver tomorrow, but she felt strangely listless and heavy.

She found she did not like the house without Agnes in it. It was far too quiet as well as too huge for just herself. Even the maid was gone for good. Agnes had given her a generous bonus and helped her line up a job with a neighbor before she had left for Colorado almost a week ago.

The past two months had been almost unreal to Sara. She had returned to California with Agnes accompanying her and since her own apartment had been closed after the plane accident, Agnes had insisted that she move into her home for the time being. Also, since her decision to resume her career, Agnes had given her no time to change her mind again. She had lined up musicians, rehearsals and finally, the new recording contract. Only last week Sara had completed work on a new album and one single. She had been kept so incredibly busy that she had had no time or energy to think and it had been exactly what she needed.

But now time hung oppressively on Sara's hands and the silence around her seemed to force upon her memories she wanted to forget. Doug.

In agitation, she chewed her lower lip and stared down at the melting ice cubes in her glass. Agnes had leased the house to a couple who would be moving in a month from now and if she were efficient, she ought to be out now looking for an apartment of her own. But like the packing that remained to be done, it did not seem urgent or important. It was as though, somehow, until Agnes and Royce's wedding was over, she hung in limbo—a never-never land where the ordinary issues of day-to-day living did not exist.

She knew what was wrong with her, of course. A sick feeling knotted her stomach just at the thought. When she returned to Denver for the wedding, she would be forced to see Doug for one last time. That was inevitable since he would, of course, be a guest at the wedding. Until that encounter was behind her, Sara felt herself to be in some sort of bondage where she was not quite free yet to get on with her own life. It was silly and made no sense, whatever, yet there it was.

She sighed heavily and stared blindly at a shrub. When she saw Doug, she must be prepared to calmly accept the news that he and Carla were engaged. By now it was bound to have happened and she had had two whole months in which to brace herself to hear it without falling apart. Even so, she wondered whether she would be able to carry it off—wondered if she would be capable of smiling and offering congratulations without giving away the slightest hint of her own turbulent emotions.

Impatient with the direction her thoughts were taking her, Sara jumped to her feet and hurried inside the house as though she could outdistance the torturous musings.

But relentlessly, they stalked her, even as she took a cab to the airport the next morning. How she wished she did not have to make this trip! But Agnes had been a special friend too many years for Sara to fail her. From somewhere deep inside she would find the necessary courage to face the coming ordeal.

During the months since she had been gone from the cabin, Sara had heard nothing about Doug. Though she received infrequent letters from Kate and Billy, it was as though there was a wall of silence around even his very name and in her own letters to them she had not had the courage to ask about him.

She could not ask Agnes either, when her friend came to meet her at the airport. She was certain that sometime during the past week Agnes had seen him, but though she waited breathlessly for some mention of him, it did not come. Instead, Agnes was filled with wedding talk and seemed to bubble over with the enthusiasm of a young first-time bride instead of a mature woman getting married for a second time. Every other sentence was punctuated with "Royce says . . ." and "Royce wants . . ." or "Royce thinks . . ."

Despite her own unhappiness, Sara laughed and felt better somehow. Agnes' high spirits were contagious. "Royce," she said teasingly, "must be a real paragon! Is there nothing he doesn't know or can't do?"

Agnes flushed as they walked side by side out to Royce's car, each of them carrying one of Sara's bags. "I'm overdoing it, huh?" she asked.

Sara laughed again and shook her head. "Not at all. I'm delighted to see you so happy. It's just that I'm still so amazed over the change in you."

Agnes grinned. "Frankly, so am I. Love is wonderful, Sara, at any age." Now she leveled an intense gaze at her young friend. "You really ought to try it sometime."

Something caught in Sara's throat and she swallowed over it with difficulty. "Maybe I will sometime," she answered as casually as she could. Pride lifted her chin and she was glad she had never told Agnes about her feelings for Doug. Pride was the only thing she had left these days, and so long as no one knew of her love for him, she could at least face the world with some semblance of dignity.

Suddenly she felt ashamed of herself. She had more than pride—much more, and she should be grateful for all she did have instead of feeling sorry for herself because one man did not happen to return that love. She had always detested whining, self-pitying people, yet that was what she was allowing herself to become! But she had no business feeling that way. She had her health back in full measure at last, wonderful friends, a future in her career. Most people would think her very fortunate indeed, and so she was!

Unconsciously, Sara squared her shoulders and her blue eyes sparkled with resolution. Tomorrow, she would sail through the wedding with a smile on her lips and peace in her heart despite the presence of Doug and Carla. Surely she had enough backbone to be able to get through a few measly hours of their company, knowing that afterward she would never need to see them again!

It was a gray, heavy day and the air was sharp and chilling. Sara was glad when they reached the car. As they drove toward the hotel where she had booked a room, she could see the snow-covered mountains in the distance. The pure white of their peaks stood out starkly against the dullness of the sky.

Agnes, too, was eyeing the sky. "Royce says it will

be snowing by tonight." She frowned with displeasure. "I just wish it would hold off until after the wedding."

"Speaking of which," Sara asked, "is there anything you want me to help you with today?"

"No. Everything's under control. You just rest up and be ready for the rehearsal tonight. It starts at seven. Do you want me to send Royce to pick you up?" She turned onto Seventeenth Street.

"Don't bother," Sara replied as they pulled up in front of the hotel. "I'll take a cab."

By six-thirty that evening she was satisfied with her appearance. She had dressed in a cranberry-red velour winter dress, the only shade of red she felt went well with her light complexion and blonde hair. Her hair, too, pleased her. It had finally grown back out to a flattering shoulder-length and now it fanned out from her face in golden waves.

A few minutes later she left the hotel. It was not a long drive to the small church were Agnes and Royce would be married tomorrow. As Sara paid off the cab driver, she felt the first snowflakes brush against her hands.

When the driver pulled away, she stood still for a few minutes, head uplifted so that the powdery flakes could caress her cheeks. For an instant a yearning, so deep in her soul that it shook her, held her spellbound. She wished, just one more time, that she could see the cabin, that she could take a long tramp through the snowy woods down to the creek. It must be beautiful just now, she thought wistfully, covered in winter finery.

But that was impossible, of course. With a heavy sigh, she pushed the thought away and turned toward the blazing lights within the church.

Slowly, she went up the steps and into the vestibule where she shed her coat and then she quietly stepped through the opened doorway into the sanctuary.

Suddenly, her heart stopped, lurched and began hammering frantically inside her breast. Clustered in a small group near the altar were Royce, Agnes, a man Sara assumed was the minister—and Doug! She had not expected to see him here tonight and the shock of it reeled her senses.

"Ah, there she is!" Royce exclaimed as he glanced up and saw her standing there. "Now we can get started."

At his words all the others turned toward Sara, including Doug. Even from such a distance, she felt the strong impact of his gaze. Her face tingled and dream-like, she moved slowly down the aisle, her own gaze flitting anywhere and everywhere except toward him. All the same, her heightened senses were acutely tuned to him, to the piercing intensity of his eyes upon her and she could feel her muscles tightening with nervous tension.

While the others greeted her, Doug's silence passed unnoticed except by Sara. Then the minister was issuing directions to them all in general and with an effort, she forced herself to pay attention.

The rehearsal was unmercifully long. Sara, accompanied by the organist, practiced the song she was to sing and then she made her way down the side aisle to the vestibule where she could then turn up the center aisle before Agnes. Besides singing, she would also be Agnes' only attendant. What had never been explained to her, however, was that Doug was to be the best man.

Finally it was over and they all went to a private club where Royce treated them to dinner. The organist and her husband, both friends of Royce's, came as well. Almost by cruel design, Doug and Sara were seated side by side at the table.

With a major effort, Sara tried to behave as though she were enjoying herself, but it was the hardest thing she had ever done in her life. Yet she could not spoil Agnes and Royce's evening by allowing the smallest hint of her agitation to show through.

If her nearness bothered Doug, however, he kept the fact well hidden. He made toasts to the bridal couple, joked and laughed and generally helped along the party atmosphere. Only toward the slight girl at his side was there a cold, strong silence. It was almost as though she were invisible.

Then the worst happened. After dinner, both the other couples got up to dance to a slow, lilting romantic tune that a combo was playing. Sara suddenly found herself alone at the table with Doug . . . an intolerable situation.

She reached for her small handbag on the table, about to make a fast retreat to the safety of the ladies' room. But before she could get out of her chair, Doug's long browned fingers covered hers.

"May I have this dance?" he asked quietly.

Sara steeled herself to look up at him. His dark eyes were unreadable as they steadily met hers, so that she could have no sense of what he was thinking or feeling.

"I . . . I don't think so," she said. Panic surged through her and she tried to withdraw her hand from beneath his.

Doug's brows crushed low over his eyes and he frowned at her. "Better reconsider," he told her. "Agnes happens to be looking our way right now. Want her to think something's wrong?"

Startled, Sara turned slightly in her chair so that she could see the dance floor and sure enough, Agnes was watching them. She gave Sara a little wave.

In defeat, Sara stood up and allowed Doug to lead

her to the dance floor. It was impossible to do otherwise if she wished to avoid an unpleasant scene as well as penetrating questions from Agnes.

She had not bargained on seeing Doug tonight, much less being required to dance with him. Now, all her afternoon resolutions about facing him with courageous indifference seemed to melt like snow beneath a hot sun as he drew her into his arms.

For a time they danced in complete silence and Sara could only pray that Doug could not hear the quick beating of her heart. She held herself stiffly, as far away from him as possible, terrified of any inflammatory body contact and she kept her eyes at a level with the knot of his somber blue necktie.

"How have you been?" Doug's low voice at last broke the tense silence between them.

"Fine . . . just fine," she replied quickly. "And you?" Briefly, she allowed her lashes to flutter upward so that she was looking at his face.

"The same," Doug replied noncommittally. His eyes seemed to bore into hers before he added, "You're looking very well."

"Thank you." Sara's voice was husky and she cleared her throat before asking, "How's Billy? Is he enjoying going to school in town?"

Doug nodded and a slight warmth lit his eyes. "He loves it. He's grown a lot since you left, too." He glanced measuringly at the crown of her head. "I'll bet he's as tall as you are now."

"I'd like to see him," Sara murmured. "Will he be coming to the wedding tomorrow?"

"Yes, he'll be there. So will Kate and Vernon. But you are also welcome to come out to the house to visit them, too, you know. Perhaps on Sunday?"

Sara shook her head. "I won't be here then. I'm flying back to L.A. late tomorrow night."

"That's too bad," Doug said politely. But he did not say it in a manner that led her to believe he meant it. In truth, Sara supposed he was relieved that she wasn't taking him up on his invitation because it meant he would not need to bother exerting himself to behave like a genial host.

The music ended and they returned to the table. Rather than face the possibility of having to dance with Doug again, Sara excused herself to the others, claiming a long day and fatigue, and then took a cab back to the hotel.

She *was* tired, but all the same it took a long time for her to fall asleep once she was in bed. Her mind refused to banish its picture of Doug tonight, unreasonably handsome in a dark business suit. She shuddered, remembering the streak of electricity that had gone through her when he had touched her while they were dancing. Now, she could even recall the clean male scent of him.

Angrily, she pounded her pillow with her fist. Why, why did she have to love him? Why couldn't she get him out of her mind for good—after all, wasn't he out of her life? But the answer, like sleep, eluded her.

By Saturday afternoon, the snowfall of the evening and early morning hours had ended. Everything wore a fresh, clean coat of white snow—tree branches, roof tops, even cars, as though a painter had just come through with a brush dipped in cream. Sara viewed the winterland scene with keen appreciation as she rode to the church.

She found Agnes and the organist in the minister's study. The organist had a box of boutonnieres in her hand. "Oh, hello." The woman smiled. "Your bouquet is over there in that box." She waved a hand toward the desk. "I'd better go give these to the men and then it will be about time to start."

After she left the room, Sara smiled at Agnes who

looked beautiful in a floor-length beige velvet gown. "Be happy," she said simply.

"Thanks," Agnes responded a little unsteadily. Then, "You'll be coming back to visit us from time to time." It was a command rather than a question. "You know that Royce thinks of you almost like a daughter the same as I do."

"I know," Sara answered, "and I will be visiting you." From beyond the door she could hear the muted strains of the organ playing and now she added, "We'd better go. You don't want to keep him waiting."

They hugged each other briefly, then left the room. Agnes' brother from Chicago had come to give her away and now he met them in the small hallway. As they turned to go toward the vestibule, Sara slipped inside a side door next to the altar and took her place near the organ.

The church was filled with guests, but Sara was scarcely aware of them. As she began to sing the sweet love song that Pete had written, her eyes were involuntarily drawn to the tall, dark man who stood on the opposite side of the altar just behind Royce.

Doug's face was grave and unreadable as he listened to her and then, miraculously, his gaze softened and became unmistakably tender. His expression twisted Sara's heart and it was beyond her to look away from him. Once again the old magic spell was there and she gave in to it, not even attempting to fight it. Her eyes moistened as she sang words of love just to him and when the song came to a close, she knew she had never sung better in her entire career. When the music ended, there was a deep hush in the room, as though everyone present had been touched by the meaning of the song.

Sara wrenched her gaze from Doug and was

suddenly aware of time and place again. Gracefully, she moved down the side aisle toward the vestibule to join Agnes and her brother. As the organist began to play again, she moved slowly up the center aisle toward the altar.

The ceremony did not take long and suddenly it was time to march out, this time with Doug at her side. Sara's hand trembled as she placed it in the crook of his arm and Doug, noticing, smiled warmly before placing his own hand briefly over hers. The brilliancy of his smile snatched at her breath and all at once, Sara felt absurdly happy.

Throughout the picture taking at the reception hall, Sara remained in a trance. Doug was constantly at her side, smiling encouragingly at her, his arm more often than not around her waist. It was a fool's paradise and it might have gone on indefinitely for Sara if Carla had not been present.

When she had a free moment, Sara had been about to cross the room to speak with Kate and Billy. But before she could do so, Carla approached her.

"You sang beautifully," she complimented Sara with a smile, "and I wanted to ask you if you'll come back and sing at Doug and my wedding? We'd consider it a great honor if you would."

Sara's bones chilled despite the heated air in the room. The joyous enchantment that had sparkled in her eyes ever since she had sung to Doug now dulled and went flat.

"And when is your wedding?" She heard herself ask in a lifeless voice.

Carla shrugged daintily. "It's not definite yet, but probably around Valentine's Day."

"Congratulations," Sara said numbly.

"Thank you." Carla's smile was bright, her voice lilting. "And *will* you sing for us as you did today?"

"I'm sorry," Sara answered through stiff lips, "but

I'll be busy on a tour in February. Now if you'll excuse me, I see Kate across the room and I'd like to speak to her."

She made good her escape, but for Sara, the remainder of the day was ruined. All her former pleasure was gone and it was difficult even to talk with Kate, Vernon and Billy. All she wanted to do was to run, hide, to be allowed to lick her wounds in private. Totally forgotten was her previous resolution to face Doug's engagement with equanimity. All her logic had abandoned her; now she was only a quivering mass of painful emotions.

When Doug came to claim her for the obligatory dance after the bride and groom had circled the room once alone, Sara was rigid in his arms.

"You're very lovely today," he whispered to her as he whirled her around.

"Thank you." Sara's voice was clipped and abrupt. She was concentrating fiercely upon not being affected by his touch, by the soft expression in his eyes, by his incredible good looks today in a black tuxedo.

"Your singing was fantastic," he said with a slight catch to his voice. "I've never heard anything more beautiful."

Sara's anger seethed within her, anger that Doug should dare to want her to sing at his wedding too after all that had happened between them. Suddenly, the bitterness spilled over. "Thank you again," she said disdainfully. "It's nice to know you think enough of my voice to want me to sing at your wedding, too. But I'm afraid I only do that for my *friends*."

Doug's eyes narrowed and he looked puzzled. "Sing at my wedding?"

"Don't pretend you don't know that Carla asked me a few minutes ago," Sara snapped.

"You turned her down?"

Sara nodded. "I appreciate the invitation," she said scornfully, "but I really don't need to line up wedding jobs, you know."

"I see." Doug was silent for a moment, then said, "That's too bad. I can't think of anything I'd like better than to have you sing at my wedding. Sure I can't change your mind?"

"I'm positive," Sara said stonily. Really, Doug had more audacity than Carla if he honestly believed he could talk her into such a thing! The music ended then and Sara jerked herself away from him quickly and walked away, beyond caring whether anyone saw the action.

An hour later Agnes and Royce left, amid a flurry of rice-throwing and good-humored jokes. Immediately afterward, Sara found her coat and purse and headed for a side door. By now her head was throbbing from the effort of smiling and pretending she was enjoying herself.

She reached the quiet of the outer hall where there was a public telephone she could use to call a cab. But suddenly, from behind her, a deep voice asked, "Are you leaving?"

Startled, she turned and met Doug's level gaze. She gave him a curt nod and wordlessly, walked over to the telephone.

"I'll drive you back to your hotel," he offered.

"That isn't necessary," she answered stiffly. "I'll just get a cab." She lifted the telephone receiver as she fished in her purse for a coin.

Doug suddenly removed the receiver from her hand and hung it up. "I'm driving you," he offered firmly, in a voice that permitted no argument. He gripped her arm tightly and guided her out the door to his parked car.

It was now late afternoon and the sky was a deep gray as though yet more snow might come by nightfall. Seated beside Doug, Sara's heart felt as leaden as the sky. Why, she wondered dismally, had he insisted on driving her back to the hotel? Why couldn't he have just left her alone?

She stared down at her hands in her lap, feeling awkward and uncomfortable over the strained silence that was between them. For the life of her, she could not think of a single thing to say.

It was some time before she happened to lift her head and glance out the window and when she did, the scenery surprised her.

"Hey!" She said sharply. "You're supposed to be taking me to the hotel!" Instead, they were on the way out of the city, traveling in the direction Sara had taken many times in the past between Denver and Lucky.

"I thought you might like to see the mountains up close," Doug said casually, "now that they're covered with snow."

"I'd love it," she snapped, "*if* I happened to have the time, which I don't. I've got a flight reservation tonight. Turn around, Doug."

"You can always take another flight tomorrow," he said with supreme nonchalance.

"You don't understand!" she exclaimed. "I *want* to catch that plane tonight!"

Doug shook his head. "You only think you do," he informed her in a maddeningly calm voice. "The mountains are gorgeous right now and Lucky Creek is beginning to ice over. Surely you want to see it before you go back."

"No, I don't!" Sara shouted. "Darn it, Doug, I don't like this game you're playing. Now turn around and take me back at once!"

"Relax," he said mildly. "You're entirely too uptight. Now just look at that view." He waved a hand, indicating the mountains toward which they were headed. "Have you ever seen anything more beautiful? I promised Billy we'd get out the sleds tomorrow. If you'll stick around for another day or so, we might even allow you to join us."

"Am I," Sara asked darkly, "being kidnapped?"

A mischievous smile flitted across Doug's lips. "You might say that," he allowed.

"Why?"

"I'm holding you for ransom." He laughed.

"What ransom?"

He shook his head again. "Oh, I'm not tipping my hand just yet. You'll find out soon enough. Now just lean back, close your eyes and relax. Is it warm enough for you?" he asked solicitously. "I can turn up the heat if you like."

"I'm quite warm enough," she retorted as she crossed her arms in disgust.

"Yes," Doug taunted, "your face is a little flushed, at that."

Sara had thought he was taking her to his house, but instead, Doug stopped in front of the cabin. At her questioning look, he merely smiled, but said nothing as he got out of the car, went around to her door and opened it.

The cabin was cold when they went inside and Sara shivered and drew her coat tighter around her. Doug immediately turned on the heat, then knelt before the fireplace. "Why don't you put on the kettle while I get a fire going?" He tossed over his shoulders. "Some coffee would be nice, don't you think?"

"Do kidnap victims make coffee?" she asked tartly.

She saw his shoulders twitch as he laughed. "They do if they want any."

Sara sighed, shed her coat and went toward the kitchen. She might as well do as he asked, she supposed. She was here against her will, but that was no reason to do without the small comforts of life.

The living room was toasty warm by the time she returned with the coffee tray. A fire blazed and hissed in the hearth, casting dark shadows against the walls. Outside, she could hear the wind whispering through the trees.

Sara placed the tray on the coffee table and sat down at one end of the sofa. Doug had shed his overcoat and the formal bow tie and now he came to sit at the opposite end of the sofa. For a long time both of them drank in silence, mesmerized by the golden flames that leaped before them.

Without warning, Doug removed the cup from Sara's hand and set it on the tray. Then he half turned so that he was facing her and now he stretched an arm along the back of the sofa. A small, teasing smile played across his lips.

"Well," he said softly, "here we are once again . . . alone together in an isolated cabin like we were once before, Sheila Starr."

Tears scalded her eyes and Sara looked away from him. "Is it fun for you . . . reminding me?" she asked bitterly. "Are you going to make yet another advance toward me so you can have the pleasure of rejecting me again?"

Abruptly, Doug moved closer. She could feel his body heat just before he buried his head in the curvature of her neck, sending small electrical shocks through her as his lips touched her skin.

"Yes," he murmured huskily, "I do intend to make advances to you. You always were irresistible to me."

"Don't!" Her voice cracked and she leaned forward. One hand went up to rub against her neck as though she could wipe away his kisses.

"Why not?" Doug leaned forward as well. One of his arms circled around her as his other hand went to her chin and slowly turned her face to meet his gaze.

"I'm hoping this time neither of us will reject the other." His eyes darkened and he looked at her intently. "I love you and I want to marry you."

Sara sucked in a sharp breath and her eyes searched his face carefully. There were no signs of teasing but, even so, she could not believe the words.

"You're engaged to Carla, remember?" She said scornfully as she tried to withdraw from his arms.

"No," he said quietly. "I'm not."

She paused in her efforts to free herself and went very still. "Not?" Her voice was weak, hardly above a whisper.

"She lied." Doug's mouth twisted into a wry smile. "Don't ask me why, unless she, like we have been, is bent on revenge, too. She knows very well I have no intentions of marrying her. Until today, I haven't seen her since you went away. So now . . . will you answer my question?"

"Question?"

"I asked you to marry me," he reminded her patiently.

"No, you didn't." Sara shook her head. "You merely stated that you wanted to marry me."

Doug gave her a little shake. "Semantics. Stop quibbling." His lips came tantalizingly close to hers. "Tell me, my love, will you sing at my wedding now? It's the ransom I demand. Otherwise I might have to hold you prisoner here forever."

"Are you sure that's what you want?" she asked wistfully. "I mean, this could just be a reaction brought about by all the wedding hoopla."

"Think so, hmm?" A light of battle flashed in his eyes and then his mouth hungrily devoured hers. Sara found herself being pressed back against the cushions, helpless beneath the assault of his kisses on her lips, her throat, her eyelids. She quivered breathlessly as his hands slid through her hair so that her head was imprisoned as he plundered her mouth once again.

When he finally released her so that she could breathe again, he grinned. "Still believe it's just a reaction from somebody else's romance?" When she shook her head, he laughed softly. "The only reason I didn't follow you to California was because Agnes told me you'd be back for her wedding. I figured I'd give you a little time to get over your anger so that hopefully by now you'd listen to me. But I'm still," he pointed out, "waiting for your answer."

"I love you, Doug," Sara said simply. "I have ever since that other night and that other cabin three years ago. But you rejected my love then and I—" she lowered her lashes to conceal the turbulent emotions in her eyes— "I guess I just can't trust your love now."

Doug sighed and surprised her by releasing her. He got to his feet and went to stand in front of the fire. "I don't blame you for hating me after that, Sara. I hated myself even more. When I first met you, I was charmed by you, by your beauty and your delightful open personality. But I had just been through several bad months . . . losing my best friend, going through legal channels to become Billy's guardian and then having Carla jilt me because of him. She had broken off with me only a couple of weeks before we met, and the last thing I was in the mood for was a commitment of any sort."

He sighed heavily and turned toward her, his eyes unwavering as they met hers. "I was completely infatuated with you, or at least that's what I told myself, and I wanted to make love to you. When you said you'd spend the weekend with me, it never dawned on me that you didn't know your way around. You were in show business for one thing and for another you agreed to the plan so quickly." He gave a light shrug to his shoulders. "I thought we'd have a pleasant weekend and go our separate ways afterward with no regrets on either side. Until that night."

He stopped and was silent for so long, Sara had to prompt him. "And that night?" Her voice was husky. "Why were you so furious with me? That's what I've never understood, Doug. Why you were so angry and so . . . so cruel."

Her question brought a look of pain to his eyes and a grim set to his mouth. "By then I knew I was falling in love with you, too, in spite of myself," he answered gruffly. "I had begun to realize that Carla had only been available, a habit. What I felt for you was so different. But I couldn't trust in love, Sara . . . just as you can't now. I had to look at the way Carla had dumped me. And there you were, a bright, young new singer with a glittering future ahead and I figured you would be even *less* inclined than Carla to settle down in marriage to a man raising a crippled child. Yes, I was angry with you!" His voice grew thick. "I was furious to discover you had never slept with a man before, yet you were freely offering yourself to me! It put pressure on me to be responsible toward you, to not just take advantage of the situation. And when you said you were doing it because you loved me, that just intensified the pressure. That's when I decided to end it so brutally. If I made you hate me enough, you'd soon forget me and find someone else. And there have been men in your life . . . I've read about you in the papers." He raked a hand through his hair and stared down at the fire again. "But I never forgot you," he ended in a hushed voice, "or stopped caring. I followed your career like the most avid of fans. I bought all your records and I even went to see you once in a live concert."

"You came to one of my concerts?" Sara asked incredulously. She got to her feet and went to stand directly behind him. "Where? And if you cared as you say you did, why didn't you come backstage?"

Doug gave a mirthless laugh and turned to stare broodingly at her. "I saw you in Chicago and you were magnificent. I kept saying to myself, 'There's my love, my princess, on that stage.' But I didn't go backstage because I was certain I would be the last man on earth you'd want to see."

"For a smart man," Sara laughed unsteadily, "that sure was dumb. You're the *only* man I've ever wanted to see."

Doug crushed her into his arms in a fierce, passionate embrace, but when his lips possessed hers at last, only tenderness and promise remained.

"I adore you, my little wood nymph," he whispered shakily. "From the moment you arrived at my cabin, I felt your magic spell weaving around me, imprisoning my heart. I could scarcely believe I was falling in love again at last . . . never dreaming it was my very own princess all the time! I knew there was something familiar about your looks and your voice, but you sure were rough on me whenever I tried to figure it out!"

Sara laughed and lovingly rubbed her thumb back and forth across his cleft chin. "I felt that my only protection was in your not knowing who I was. I didn't want your scorn . . . or your pity."

"Pity?" He exploded. "For what? A limp that soon went away? I didn't pity you . . . I pitied myself. I was afraid you were going to marry Royce. I was completely surprised when he told me he was going to marry Agnes. Sara—" Anxiety coated his voice. "Are you sure you want me, darling? I mean, Billy and I do come as a package deal."

"A two-for-one bonus." She grinned. "I always did like a good bargain."

Doug grinned too, obviously relieved. "And you'll continue your career, too," he told her firmly.

"You've got a tremendous talent that must be shared with the world. We'll work something out so that I'll be able to travel with you some of the time."

"Must I?" she asked dreamily. "I was thinking about retiring and having five or six babies and—"

"You little temptress!" he growled as he drew her close to him again. "With talk like that, I'll soon forget it wasn't *our* wedding today! You're marrying me just as soon as we can get the license, understand?"

Sara nodded obediently. "And in the meantime?" she murmured.

"In the meantime, I'm going to need a lot of reassurance that you really do love me as much as I love you," he told her.

"Yes? And how can I manage that?"

There was a distinct gleam in Doug's eyes just before he lifted her into his arms and carried her to the sofa. "I'll show you," he said softly.

And he did.

Silhouette Romance

IT'S YOUR OWN SPECIAL TIME

Contemporary romances for today's women.
Each month, six very special love stories will be yours
from SILHOUETTE. Look for them wherever books are sold
or order now from the coupon below:

$1.50 each

__#61 WHISPER MY NAME Michaels	__#80 WONDER AND WILD DESIRE Stephens
__#62 STAND-IN BRIDE Halston	__#81 IRISH THOROUGHBRED Roberts
__#63 SNOWFLAKES IN THE SUN Brent	__#82 THE HOSTAGE BRIDE Dailey
__#64 SHADOW OF APOLLO Hampson	__#83 LOVE LEGACY Halston
__#65 A TOUCH OF MAGIC Hunter	__#84 VEIL OF GOLD Vitek
__#66 PROMISES FROM THE PAST Vitek	__#85 OUTBACK SUMMER John
__#67 ISLAND CONQUEST Hastings	__#86 THE MOTH AND THE FLAME Adams
__#68 THE MARRIAGE BARGAIN Scott	__#87 BEYOND TOMORROW Michaels
__#69 WEST OF THE MOON St. George	__#88 AND THEN CAME DAWN Stanford
__#70 MADE FOR EACH OTHER Afton Bonds	__#89 A PASSIONATE BUSINESS James
__#71 A SECOND CHANCE ON LOVE Ripy	__#90 WILD LADY Major
__#72 ANGRY LOVER Beckman	__#91 WRITTEN IN THE STARS Hunter
__#73 WREN OF PARADISE Browning	__#92 DESERT DEVIL McKay
__#74 WINTER DREAMS Trent	__#93 EAST OF TODAY Browning
__#75 DIVIDE THE WIND Carroll	__#94 ENCHANTMENT Hampson
__#76 BURNING MEMORIES Hardy	__#95 FOURTEEN KARAT BEAUTY Wisdom
__#77 SECRET MARRIAGE Cork	__#96 LOVE'S TREACHEROUS JOURNEY Beckman
__#78 DOUBLE OR NOTHING Oliver	__#97 WANDERER'S DREAM Clay
__#79 TO START AGAIN Halldorson	__#98 MIDNIGHT WINE St. George
	__#99 TO HAVE, TO HOLD Camp

$1.75 each

__#100 YESTERDAY'S SHADOW Stanford	__#106 THE LANCASTER MEN Dailey
__#101 PLAYING WITH FIRE Hardy	__#107 TEARS OF MORNING Bright
__#102 WINNER TAKE ALL Hastings	__#108 FASCINATION Hampson
__#103 BY HONOUR BOUND Cork	__#112 WHISPER WIND Stanford
__#104 WHERE THE HEART IS Vitek	__#113 WINTER BLOSSOM Browning
__#105 MISTAKEN IDENTITY Eden	__#114 PAINT ME RAINBOWS Michaels
__#109 FIRE UNDER SNOW Vernon	__#115 A MAN FOR ALWAYS John
__#110 A STRANGER'S WIFE Trent	__#116 AGAINST THE WIND Lindley
__#111 WAYWARD LOVER South	__#117 MANHATTAN MASQUERADE Scott

Introducing
First Love from
Silhouette Romances for teenage girls to build their dreams on.

They're wholesome, fulfilling, supportive novels about every young girl's dreams. Filled with the challenges, excitement— and responsibilities—of love's first blush, *First Love* paperbacks prepare young adults to stand at the threshold of maturity with confidence and composure.

Introduce your daughter, or some young friend to the *First Love* series by giving her a one-year subscription to these romantic originals, written by leading authors. She'll receive two NEW $1.75 romances each month, a total of 24 books a year. Send in your coupon now. **There's nothing quite as special as a First Love.**

Silhouette **Romance**

15-Day Free Trial Offer
6 Silhouette Romances

6 Silhouette Romances, free for 15 days! We'll send you 6 new Silhouette Romances to keep for 15 days, absolutely free! If you decide not to keep them, send them back to us. You pay nothing.

Free Home Delivery. But if you enjoy them as much as we think you will, keep them by paying the invoice enclosed with your free trial shipment. We'll pay all shipping and handling charges. You get the convenience of Home Delivery and we pay the postage and handling charge each month.

Don't miss a copy. The Silhouette Book Club is the way to make sure you'll be able to receive every new romance we publish before they're sold out. There is no minimum number of books to buy and you can cancel at any time.

This offer expires April 30, 1982

Silhouette Book Club, Dept. **SB117B**
120 Brighton Road, Clifton, NJ 07012

Please send me 6 Silhouette Romances to keep for 15 days, absolutely free. I understand I am not obligated to join the Silhouette Book Club unless I decide to keep them.

NAME_____

ADDRESS_____

CITY_____ STATE_____ ZIP_____